TIME OF DECISION

Ray Mallin returned from the stars to find his home-planet Mars fallen shockingly into decay and apathy. Once Mars had been the great hope of the Solar System, where men came out from Earth to test their strength and adaptiveness on a harsh new world— now the progress of mankind had passed Mars by, and she had become a second-class planet, her Mars-born humans only dead-end mutations.

But Ray Mallin had no time to ponder the desperate situation of his world, for as soon as he landed he was abducted by agents of one of the star-empires and was put through a brutal torture session to make him talk about his last voyage. Still recovering from his wounds, he sought guidance from his aged Martian mentor—and found treachery, intrigue, danger ... and a secret that could affect the entire future of mankind!

Born Under Mars

by

JOHN BRUNNER

ACE BOOKS, INC.
1120 Avenue of the Americas
New York, New York 10036

John Brunner has also written:

I

I WOULD TELL it as it happened to me. But I am no longer as I was when it happened. At least, though, I can remember when the change began—to the hour, almost to the minute.

There was the bare room lit by a single high fluorescent yellowed with age. It held some chairs. One of them was of stone, hand-carved, weighing about a quarter of a ton. They had lashed me to it because even in Martian gravity no one could have moved dragging such a load. To me, as a Martian, it was the weight of death itself.

I was thinking a lot of death because of what Thoder had taught me—what I was learning after so many years was of importance. I was afraid of the last thing he said, in his rusty hollow voice: "There is always an escape, Ray, even if it is only through the wall at the end of life."

But this escape I did not wish to take. Had there been a reason, had I known why these men were doing to me— what they were doing—I might have put his lesson into effect.

The lack of a reason brought to mind an earlier teaching of Thoder's, when he said, "Consolation is armour." I had such consolation; I knew that whatever my interrogators wanted from me they weren't getting it. But it was a fragile shield against a nerve-whip. I could claim small credit for not giving information I didn't possess.

Still, I leaned on that support for all I was worth. I wanted to recall this time. The four who were torturing me were wearing privacy screens and their voices were filtered. If I sought clues to their identity—and I did, with all the blazing raw agony of my nerves—I must miss nothing.

I had weakened at the beginning and thought of another teaching Thoder showed me, not understood till now, with his little bead-on-a-string: how to let time go lax and speed the ball of consciousness towards the future. This was easy —after all, it was the process of sleep. Enduring, I had come on the frail staff of my sole consolation to considering the reverse: the tautening of time so that the bead stopped, the *now* froze. Yet I burned so, I burned so under my skin!

If I live, I will find Thoder and beg forgiveness . . .

No, I could not summon the mental resources to slow time; accordingly I could seize only the intervals between blasts of agony to look, listen, smell, feel and remember these men.

At first I had thought "slavers!" In spite of every official denial, rumours about kidnapping for slavery went on spreading. Most of the accusations were against the Tyranny of Centaurus, of course. Officially, only Earthmen had views, individually, while Earth was nonpartisan, but most Earthmen's sympathies lay with the Bears.

Ironical! Me, Ray Mallin, brought to a typical Earthman's attitude!

My mind was wandering. I had wasted irreplaceable seconds. I snatched it back to the knowledge that the interval since the last nerve-whipping was exceptionally long, and I had a chance to concentrate again.

Accents? They speak Anglic fluently. But I speak the lingua spatia *of both Centaurs and Bears with equally good accent and vocabulary, so these people could be . . .*

Pointless. Listen instead to what is said, I told myself as though I were Thoder.

The man in the middle chair of the group of three facing me snapped, "One more time, I said!"

The man apart from the others, holding the nerve-whip,

raised his instrument. I tensed, but the leader shook his head. "Try it without the whip," he directed. "The pain may be keying in a hypnotic cover-story."

I tried not to show relief, as the last of the men turned to face me—at least, the shapeless mass of his privacy screen hunched to suggest the action—and said in his cajoling voice, "Ray Mallin! Your last voyage! Think back and tell us how it began!"

Should I tell it this time more fully, supplying extra details—? I rejected the temptation. I was near to convincing these people I was speaking truth, near to victory, near to escape and to revenge. To waste the advantage was futile. Anyhow, what difference did elaboration make? The substance was still the unvarnished truth.

My last voyage but one had taken me as far as Durrith. I had never travelled much in Centaur space before, but I'd seen most of the interesting worlds in the Bear sphere of influence, and I'd finally grown sick of the discrepancy between Earth's official neutrality propaganda and what everyone knew to be the preference underlying it. I was afraid to fall into the stereotyped assumptions that would make people think I was what my papers called me: an Earth citizen.

Not that I thought of it in terms of "being afraid" until later, when I'd grown more honest.

I learned the very hard way that I'd swallowed much of that propaganda, despite my resentment of it. It implied things were much the same whether you went north or south of the Old System. They weren't. The third time I was cocky with the Chief Officer of the tub I was aboard—he was an aristocrat claiming family connections with the Tyrant himself—I was dumped. On Durrith. If a Centaur crewman had done the same thing he would probably have been dumped without the courtesy of having a planet put under his feet first, but for the only time in my life that I could recall I was grateful for my official nationality. An advantage of being an Earthman was that in whichever sphere of influence you were you knew that the other side was temporarily supporting you. Not that I could thank Earth's scheming politicians for this incidental benefit—it resulted merely from the strategic location of the Old System between two great power-blocs.

However, for whatever reason, the Centaur officer had been constrained to show me the lock on a habitable planet. I was on Durrith, with half a trip's pay and no prospects.

At first I wasn't particularly alarmed. I headed for Traffic Control at Durrith Main Port, and invested part of my ready cash in getting drinking-acquainted with the port controllers. This technique had worked for me before, on Goldstar; that time, I was unofficially notified of an engineer's post on a freighter, and the only drawback was that if I showed my nose on Goldstar again the local crewmen's fraternity would chop it off. Not that I cared. The fraternity hadn't copied the progressive unions closer to the Old System and recognised Martian nationality. Until they did . . .

Anyhow, this was irrelevant. On Durrith, as on other worlds south of Sol in Centaur space, they didn't have fraternities. But they did have patronage.

Three weeks on Durrith, no sign of a berth, I was debating whether to buy passage home—which smacked of defeat—or take the cheaper course, against all my principles, and have the local Earth consul ship me home DTS (Distressed Terrestrial Subject), with the injury-worsening insult of having to spend a year in government service on my return to work off the dead horse. To work, without pay, for *Earth!* The idea revolted me.

I'd spun out my cash as far as I could by helping in a bar on the port—discovering that what went over with the Bears failed miserably here—when Lugath turned up.

Lugath was so unlike the Centaur officers I'd met until then that, had he not been commanding a ship under Centaur registry, I'd hardly have credited his claim to citizenship in this sector. For one thing, he showed harrassment, which Centaurs regarded as undignified. For another, he addressed me as a fellow man. And he came rapidly to the point.

"They tell me you can handle four-space drivers."

I produced my certificates. Of course, the fact that they were heavily overstamped with Bear merit endorsements had weighed against me in Centaur space. Still, they were what I had—and they were good.

I half-expected Lugath to curl his lip and walk away on seeing so many Bear stamps. Instead, he merely commented, "You've served mostly in Bear space, I see."

I shrugged and nodded—as Thoder would have said, to no point.

"What brings you this side?"

"A four-space freezer!" I snapped, and immediately regretted it. That was the kind of answer I'd given the Chief Officer of that same freezer once too often, and if I didn't watch my tongue I'd lose another job the same way before it was offered.

Lugath frowned impatiently. "What was that?"

"A Spica-class refrigeration ship—sir." The last word followed late. "They dumped me because I was too ready to talk back to the Chief. But I can handle any four-space drivers you care to show me."

Lugath hesitated, but not for the reason I was anticipating. He said at length, "In that case you may not wish to return so quickly to the Old System—"

I leaned forward. This was miraculous! Right now I wanted out of Centaur space, and I didn't care if I never came back. "Earth?" I demanded. "Or Mars?"

He gave me a strange look, at the back of which was something I only identified a long time later as alarm. He said, "Mars, naturally!"

And "naturally" was right. Earth was far too wary to allow foreign vessels to broach the air of the home planet. I was afraid my spur-of-the-moment error would put him off, but he gave me the job.

His ship was as far out of the ordinary as her master. She was a conversion job. The hull was that of a Deneb-class ladyboat, half freighter and half liner, but the engines were cruiser-type, stripped to essentials to cram them into the available space. With a hull of such low mass to shift, they gave a velocity equal to a crack luxury liner's. To forestall my inevitable curiosity Lugath made an offhand reference to picking them up cheap out of a wreck. That yarn rang hollow, but I was too afraid for my job to pester him with questions.

Most of the time the engines threatened to leave the hull behind. I spent the voyage literally sleeping with them, a stress-alarm rigged by my hammock to wake me if anything went wrong. It did, frequently, and I came to wonder whether Lugath's regular engineer had suffered a breakdown from the strain, but I didn't ask after him, either. We made Mars without disaster, and Lugath paid me off with a bonus, something else I'd not have expected from a Centaur.

Aside from the anomalous drivers and Lugath's cordiality —for a Centaur; if he'd been Bear or even Earthborn I'd have classed him as pompous and haughty—the trip was unremarkable.

And that was what was troubling my interrogators.

My words died in silence. I waited. Finally the leader of the four gave a veiled shrug and gestured to the whipper. As the control of the weapon was thumbed to maximum, I strove to do as Thoder had shown me and make time accelerate, make my private "now" outrun the onset of the agony.

I was too slow, but in any case I hardly felt the pain. It was so violent I blacked out. My last conscious thought was a memory of Thoder's gentle *tsk-tsk* over a disappointing pupil.

II

SUFFOCATING . . .

I struggled against the reflex of fright, attempting to look back on this moment of waking from a calmer period ahead, explaining to myself what was terrifying me. It is the effect experienced in dreams when one thinks, "I drown, swimming with my face below water," and knows simultaneously that the flow of air is stopped by a soft pillow, so that the head rolls and the dream passes.

Not that I, a Martian, had ever actually swum in water.

I thought at first it was dust choking me—my mouth and throat were harsh-dry with soreness like sand-strangulation. But this was wrong. What lay weighty and oppressive on me, smothering my face and crowding my lungs, was thick damp air. I was giddy from hyperoxia. The remedy was to cease breathing for a while. Why had I been breathing so deeply? I looked to the soreness of my throat and found the dying tensions of strained muscles. I had been shouting, perhaps screaming, from remembered terror.

Thoder would say: "A man binds time over millions of years—are you then to be frightened of Timurlane, Tibbetts and Tovarenko?"

Not breathing, I felt, measured, analysed. The air, first. Wherever I was, it was a rich and foreign place. The measure of air on Mars is by altitude-feet of Earth-normal, taking units of a thousand from sea-level to one hundred, or Martian ground-normal. Arbitrary, but close enough. I was used to breathing at ten, like all Martians. Here, the pressure and humidity combined to make an estimate difficult, but I reckoned two, or three at the most. No wonder I had thought of suffocation; no wonder I felt oxygen-nausea as well as the fading agony of the nerve-whippings I'd endured.

Also the place I lay. A bed. I moved, testing my assumptions, and found answer yes. A bed with nulgee flotation instead of springs. I had been in one once, at an expensive house of ill fame on Charigol. I lay on it naked, on my back, one arm on my belly, one outflung at right angles to my shoulder and still not reaching the edge. Wide, this bed. Like all Martians I am lank and tall.

I breathed once more, slowly, ventilating a quarter of my lungs, and opened my eyes. I saw two people. They—and I—were in a room of water-green and gold, its one-way windows letting in the sun of early morning or late afternoon. I knew an east-west axis, therefore. My spirits rose. The place was decorated with great vases full of bronze-petalled sandflowers, whose outermost fronds stirred in the upward draught of the dry air-curtains guarding them from deliquescence in an Earth-moist environment. The walls were panelled with handwoven sandreeds, glistening a little because they too had to be protected against moisture and were sealed in a thin coat of plastic.

So: even before looking at the two people, I knew something of them—if this place were their own, or chosen by them from other possible places. Though no one could have mistaken them for Martians, still they accepted where they were, and did not try to disguise reality with masks.

A tentative deduction followed: kindly disposed to me. In plainer terms, rescuers . . . ?

Closer to me, at the edge of the bed, a girl. She was like a dwarf to me, as were most Earthfolk, but not stunted as they usually seemed—only miniaturised by the fierce gravity. She was graceful, with dark hair tied on the nape of her neck. Her face was golden, a trifle broader than oval, and from it eyes like jet stabbed out to search mine. She wore something the colour of the sandflower petals—shimmering bronze—and it rustled silkily as she bent forward.

Behind her, at her shoulder, a man: they would say *tall* on Earth, but to me squat and almost bloated. Hair light in colour, pressed down into compact spiral curls above his square pale face. He wore Earthside clothing of dark blue and black. One big spade-fingered hand rested on the arm of the girl, and to me it was like the jaws of a mechanical shovel gripping soft flesh.

"He's awake, Peter," the girl said in a voice like violins. It was curious to notice how much deeper, more thrilling, the sound was here in a densely pressurised room than what I was used to. But I would never be seduced by environmental accidents. It was the first step to the lie about women in the dark. People are alike, but never "all the same".

The man hunched as she had done, his other great hand spread on the high-line of the bed's nulgee frame, supported oddly in mid-air—and yet not so oddly to me, thinking of this air as a dense medium such as they tell me one finds in an ocean—and asked, "Are you well enough to talk now?"

I nodded.

"Do you remember what happened?"

I would remember until my dying day. But Thoder had advised, "Questions imply answers. The interrogator gives away as much as he learns." So I chose to shake my head.

"You're in the penthouse of Grand Canal Apartments," the man Peter told me. "You've been here the better part of a day. We found you lying in the dust on a street-corner near the Old Temple, almost drowned. You'd been nerve-whipped."

How did they know? Were *these* two of my interrogators? Hearing all four speak, I'd thought none was a woman, but filters, sound-shifters . . . I thought of my nakedness, and how Thoder had explained the way to read a lie in the tautening of a muscle remote from the face. But I asked how they knew.

"At first we thought you were drunk," the girl said. "You weren't. Then we thought you might have Larchman's disease. But you had no fever."

"Sober, unconscious, no fever," Peter said. "No visible injuries, yet you could hardly bear to be touched. You'd been nerve-whipped, all right."

"Drowning?" I said.

Peter's quick answer told me that despite being no Martian he understood life's harshness on my planet. He said, "Not maskless. But dust had shifted into the exhalation pipe and leaked past the valve. We heard you coughing from it."

"And you?" I said.

They exchanged glances, as if they had hoped I would reveal something else before I challenged them—cursed my attackers, perhaps, and given a clue to their identity. To understand fully why I did not waste the energy, they'd have needed to be born on Mars—or, I should say, *under* it, for our last shackle to Earth consists in the oxygen demands of the developing embryo, and pregnancy must be passed in an environment pressurised to zero or even minus one. There are few of us; perhaps the compulsion to spend three-sevenths of a year suffocating underground partly explains that fact.

But their acceptance of things as they were followed fast. The man said, "This is Lilith Choy, and I'm Peter Nizam. From Earth, of course."

"Of course." There was more irony in my response than I'd intended. "And you know who I am?"

Once more, the exchange of glances. Peter said finally, "If the papers you were carrying are your own, you're Ray Mallin. You're a four-space drive engineer, and we rather gather that you've been around enough to have acquired enemies."

"So you didn't think it strange to find me left for dead on the corner of a street?"

The reaction was unmistakable. They had hoped, for some reason, that I would take longer to regain all my faculties, and they were put out to find me putting keen-edged questions to them already. Lilith answered in a distracted fashion.

"Well—we are strangers on Mars."

"You informed the police?"

She drew back. Peter said sharply, "Are you afraid that we did? Are you a criminal?"

"No. But as my body has told you, even if my papers do not, I'm a Martian, and we have our own ways of arranging matters."

It was a trouble-saver that the screened interrogators had not taken or destroyed my papers. I could have got others easily, but they would have lacked the many merit stamps the Bears had added lately.

"Yes," Lilith said. "We—uh—we'd been told so. That was why we didn't notify the police."

"No one but us," Peter supplemented, "knows that you're here."

"I acknowledge obligation," I said reluctantly. I had to—it was custom, and they had saved my life and not done the thing I did not wish—but I hoped sternly they had not also been told the constraint under which the acknowledgement put me. To shift the focus of attention, I sat up and looked my body over quickly before sliding to the bed's edge and then to the floor. From the true commanding height of Martian stature I looked down on them, dwarfs closer to the stunting gravity-sink of Sol.

"May I have my clothes, and my belongings?"

The girl looked all the way up to my head, as though she had not integrated my length stretched on the bed with the soon-to-be-seen vertical equivalent of it, and her eyes widened a little. She said, "Yes, of course. I'll fetch them."

As she went, quick and graceful across the reedmat floor, to open a closet in an adjacent room and bring my gear, the man said hesitantly, "Will you take food? Will you not rest a while? The whipping must have been savage to make you unconscious."

"Thank you, but I have business to attend to," I said.

"With the—people—who gave you your whipping?" he suggested.

"On Mars one does not make such inquiries," I rebuked him. He flushed a little.

14

"Yes, I'm sorry. We were told that too, and I forgot. A tradition stemming from the early days, isn't it? When the only thing a man had to call his own might be a secret."

"Has anyone anywhere ever owned more than that?" I said.

The girl came back with my clothes, and I got into them. They had been laundered, and smelt fresh and clean despite the heavy damp air. Talking, I had drawn more breaths than I should have done; I made the actions of dressing vigorous to wash out the excess oxygen in my blood.

The girl Lilith made the same proposals as Peter had: to rest longer, to eat with them. I shook my head, checking my papers, looking over my mask before going on the road. They had serviced it for me, which was a kindness, and the meter on the reservoir stood hard over to "full". I felt weary from the exhaustion that followed the whipping, but I had rested well and in another day or two would be recovered.

"You're leaving straight away?" Peter said.

"Yes." I buckled the mask, held the facepiece ready to put on when I left the pressurised volume, and looked at him.

"Wait." He was almost embarrassed. "Ah—a moment ago you said you were obligated to us, didn't you?"

Someone had told him the custom. My nape prickled. He was going on, despite a warning nudge from Lilith. "Well, I don't like to take advantage, you understand, but it so happens that there is something you might do to help us in return, and by saying that you—you sort of committed yourself. Isn't that the Martian tradition?"

I could not deny the truth of this; it would be to cut my throat as a Martian. All turned now on whether the thing he wanted me to do was relevant or random. I hoped vainly for something petty and routine: a request to smuggle, possibly. Often, I'd been asked to bring in perfumes and cosmetics of which only ersatz versions were cheaply available on Mars, and this girl Lilith was beautiful for all her tininess, and—

And living in the penthouse of Grand Canal Apartments, with pressurisation at two thousand feet Earth-normal, they could pay the duty on anything they chose.

"What do you wish?" I said.

"Well, you're a spaceman, so presumably"—a vague gesture—"you go to the port here, you chat with other spacemen . . ."

A sense of doom grew in my mind.

"About three days ago a Centaur ship put in from Durrith. She's still on the port, or was this morning. She's called the *Hippodamia*, and she looks like a ladyboat but very probably isn't. We'd appreciate being told of any scandal, rumours, gossip—*anything*—about her which the people around the port are giving out with."

III

DURING THE next few seconds, I came within radar-range of breaking faith with myself as a Martian.

Peter had said, "We'd appreciate being told of scandal, rumours, gossip, the people around the spaceport are giving out with." I was not "a person around the port"—I was a space engineer. Also since my landing, my homecoming, I'd not been around the port at all; it smacked too much of intrusion from elsewhere, especially of intrusion from Earth. For ninety-nine out of every living hundred of our species, Mars signified "interstellar terminal of Old System" and not a planet with its own citizens, its own culture, traditions, customs having the effective force of law. So I'd not spoken with anybody about Lugath's ship since I signed off and headed into the city, thankful to be clear of Centaur jurisdiction.

But Peter and Lilith had seen my papers; they must have noticed the Centaur stamps concluding the long line of Bear stamps, page after page; they must have realised that the date/time of planetfall after my last trip coincided precisely with that of the ship in which they were interested, even if they hadn't recognised Lugath's signature scrawled almost illegibly in permink across the base of the discharge block.

I studied the face of both man and girl, and wrote my best estimate of their thoughts under those faces, like captions on pictures in a personality test such as Thoder used to administer to me. I assigned to the girl: *Peter, we know he*

*was on that ship! Why are you telling him straight out
that we want information?* And to Peter: *I've heard about
the fierce honour of Martians. Their honesty is something
which they claim sets them above Centaurs, Bears and
Earthfolk alike. I'm gambling on it.*

I said finally, "Tell me one thing before I answer you.
Was it sheer chance that led you to find me, drowning in
the dust of the street?"

There was an interval of indecision. During it, Lilith took
a smokehale from a pocket of her robe and set it to her
finely shaped lips. I had to conquer my Martian reaction
to the gesture, reminding myself there was oxygen here
enough to support a bonfire if someone decided to light it.
But now I knew she smoked, I lost much of my original
sense of being attracted to her physically. It was so irre-
sponsible a habit even with inexhaustible natural oxygen to
hand.

"It was partly chance," Peter said when he had chosen
his words. "We had been told that a Martian was aboard
the ship in which we're interested. The Old Temple is at the
heart of the city. We—"

The girl chimed in in a clear, decision-taken tone. She
said, "We were looking for you, but we didn't know it was
you we were looking for."

"Uh—what she means is," Peter began, "that we—"

"What she means is what she says." I gave him a puzzled
glance; Thoder had once had a pupil so proud of his pre-
cocity he kept jumping in with needless glosses on plain
statements, and this was what I was reminded of.

How they oscillated, these two! Closer to my home they
might be, in space at least, but in attitude they were further removed than any Centaur or Bear I'd ever met. Moments ago, I'd imagined the girl to be the more muddled-
minded of the pair. Now here was Peter appearing to be
far less clearheaded than she.

I gave up my attempts to resolve that particular para-
dox, and made a one-handed gesture of invitation to them
that they should continue with any questions they wished.

For all that he had acted so as to indicate his trust in
Martian honesty, Peter was now the hesitant one. It irri-
tated me, I confess. I might so easily have taken refuge in

Earth-type casuistry, walked out about my own business behind the screening half-truth that I knew no gossip about
the Centaur ship from anyone at the port—and yet this also
was only half a truth, for the fact that the screened interrogators of last night and Peter and Lilith too were so concerned with my last voyage hinted at enormous matters
beyond my scope.

I would have to be watchful and suspicious. That they
had found me soon enough to save my life shadowed a
possible link between them and the four men of last night;
it could be direct, or else a fortuitous result of a common
quest. I might have a quest in common with these two
myself, now, or alternatively I might have set myself a
mission of vengeance against them. I must be very cautious.

I must, in short, learn from them as much as they already
knew about my last voyage, because certainly it was something I had not noticed, being preoccupied with engines
which threatened to break loose from the hull. Then I must
choose a path for action.

Lilith said composedly, "Shall we sit down? If the matter
is going to come into the open, it'll take some while to talk
it through properly."

"There's no question of talking it through," Peter countered.
"I'm merely taking advantage—unfairly or not—of what our
friend committed himself to."

"He wants to know why we're inquiring about this particular ship."

"And I'm not proposing to tell him." Peter pushed his
thick powerful fingers through his dense hair. "There's no
set scale for discharge of obligations here, as far as I'm
aware, but saving a man's life might be expected to count
for a lot. Am I right?" He shot a glance at me.

"Earthmen have a random scale of values," I answered.
"You have prized things that can't be eaten, breathed or
worn."

"That's true enough," he conceded. "On Earth, a man's
life is likely to be traded for something absurd, like a nug-
get of gold. Here, you're more likely to kill for a cylinder
of oxygen or a flask of water."

"Who said anyting about killing?" Lilith demanded, seeming frightened at the directness of the challenge. Once

more they were playing this rôle-reversal game, leader becoming subordinate. I wondered if it was a deliberate pattern, designed to confuse an ignorant provincial like myself with a smokescreen of Earthside sophistication, hinting at influences too subtle for me to detect.

If it were, it wouldn't work.

"Shall we come to the point?" Peter suggested. "For reasons not connected with the obligation you've acknowledged, we have saved your life. We didn't know you were the Martian who had shipped with the vessel we're investigating until we found your papers and saw the last discharge stamp. Knowing, now, we are being blunt about asking, in the hope that you'll comply with your planetary traditions."

"I'll tell you what I can," I said.

When I'd finished, there was a pause.

"There's nothing in what he's said to make somebody nerve-whip him," Lilith commented eventually.

"We don't know that the whipping was connected," Peter countered, and turned to me. "Was it?"

"You asked about the voyage," I said stonily.

Lilith snapped her tiny fingers, the sound enormously loud in the heavy air. "If the whipping is connected, then the important thing is: what became of the man he replaced?" She was shaking with sudden tension.

Peter saw implications that escaped me, though I expected I would figure them out later. He jolted forward on his chair.

"Do you know what happened to him?" he demanded.

"I was told he'd fallen sick," I said. I was getting tired of this; I was also hungry, and there was a hint of annoyance at the back of my mind that I should have bound myself to this interrogation, not less difficult to bear than last night's even if the nerve-whip was lacking.

"An astonishing coincidence," Lilith said coldly, getting to her feet. "Peter, I think you leaned too hard on this theoretical Martian honesty."

"It falls rather patly, I agree." His eyes were on me, showing worry; they were pale blue, as I hadn't previously ascertained.

"In that case . . ." Lilith took another smokehale and drew on it nervously.

"In that case, who whipped him?" Peter supplied.

"There are two possibilities, aren't there?" she muttered. I tensed a little. They were skilful at parrying my own probes, but now they were under strain from some source I could only guess at—thinking, I imagined, that they had revealed their involvement to someone who was telling lies and in fact did know whatever secret surrounded the last voyage of Lugath's ship. I might get a glimpse past their screens.

But neither of them referred more directly to the "two possibilities", and after a brief wait I spoke loudly.

"I consider I've done what you asked for, and the obligation is charged."

"Not so fast," Peter said, rising with a grim expression. Standing, the girl was only at head-height to me in my chair, but he was—as I have said—tall by Earthside standards, and now he scowled down at me.

"This is the trouble with fixed rules of conduct, isn't it?" he said. "Absolute honesty, absolute honour . . . Along with them, one absorbs clues to the breach of them. I don't possess the clues you've learned since childhood, so without them I can only provoke you to test your consistency. You admit you were aboard that ship of—what's his name?—of Captain Lugath's. Since you came home, someone's captured you and nerve-whipped you, then left you for dead. The usual aftermath of a routine voyage? I think not. You must know there was something extraordinary about the ship—its crew, its cargo, or its passengers. All the way from Durrith to Earth you had a chance to observe what was going on, yet you maintain you noticed nothing peculiar apart from the exceptionally powerful drivers you were given to nurse. You'll pardon my Earthside boorishness, but I find that hard to credit. You're not a stupid man according to your trade certificates. Also it strikes me as improbably convenient that when Lugath's engineer—ah—*fell sick* on Durrith he should find waiting and available a qualified substitute, not a Centaur national as one would expect, but an Earth national."

"A Martian!" I snapped.

"Yes, I'm sorry." His eyes narrowed fractionally; I read this as triumph at having breached my defences, and cursed my touchiness. "A *Martian!*"

"But there's nothing much we can do if he is lying," Lilith said.

"No, of course there isn't," Peter rapped. "We don't want to degrade ourselves, take the risk of insulting a genuinely honourable man, and perhaps make an enemy needlessly. So we offer him thanks for his co-operation and—and raise one more point before we part from him."

"Which is?" I muttered.

"You said you considered the obligation discharged. Correction. What I asked you to do was bring us gossip from the port. There were others in the crew besides yourself, who may have been both more observant and less closemouthed. What you have described of your own experience aboard the ship is welcome, but *not* what I asked for in the first place."

Casuistical is an Earthside word, I thought, and resigned myself to the truth of what he said and the stupidity that had trapped me.

He said, beginning to smile, "Another drawback of absolute codes, I think: they're like levers for those who don't subscribe to them. I look forward to seeing you again and talking further about this."

I rose and stood scowling at him, wondering how in the cosmos I could both avoid picking up gossip which I'd be compelled to bring back to him and carry out a search for the screened interrogators who had whipped me last night. It was then, as he hunted for and handed to me a slip of card bearing his name, address and comweb code, that I finally connected up an anomalous pattern-breaking fact I'd had jingling about in memory ever since Durrith.

By a slip of attention I'd happened to ask Lugath whether he was bound for Earth or Mars—when I knew perfectly well no ship under Centauran registry would be allowed to broach Earth's air.

Ships under Earth registry, of course, *were* allowed to. No wonder Lugath's face had betrayed that spasm of what I now realised to have been alarm! No wonder he behaved unlike any Centaur officer I'd previously served with!

(Though I had to grant my experience was limited to a single voyage.)

Lugath had been afraid that I had recognised him for what he was: an Earthman posing as a Centaur, commanding a ship that was not what it seemed in some fashion more important than simply having cruiser's engines in a Deneb hull.

IV

BUT THIS WAS NOT the thought which filled my mind as I emerged from Grand Canal Apartments, snugging my mask to my face against the thin natural air and the dry bitter wind of evening. It was a faint peevish resentment at the drag of obsolete habit: the notion of calibrating oxygen partial pressure in terms of another planet's atmosphere after literally centuries, in modern times when the heralds claimed to be able to trace upwards of twelve Martian-born generations within a single continuing family. We might have trimmed it to a bare number—two, five, ten—but the old qualification still stood in black symbols across the face of every pressure meter on the planet: "Thousands of feet above sea-level."

And how many millions of miles from any sea?

Gradually, as I adjusted to conditions more normal for my metabolism, I freed myself of this irritating obsession. I began to be able to reason and plan. I also became increasingly aware how silly I had been to decline Peter and Lilith's offer of food and longer rest; I was terribly weak even though the whipping I had sustained was almost a whole day in the past. My guts rumbled, giving back swallowed air from the apartment I had left, forcing me to bulge my cheeks and divert five or six burps into the exhalation tube of my mask. Thus futilely occupied for a moment, I surveyed my surroundings.

Not even I would call my planet beautiful. Rolling red-brown plains, shifting dunes, hills hardly higher than the dunes, darkling sky, the moons petty blinking lights, the native plants majestic rather than handsome—even the famous sandflowers—the winds weak but harsh like much-diluted acid, half the people disliking or even detesting the remainder.

Yet I would never call it ugly, either. Stark. Plain. What would one call knotted hands scarred by the preference for love over beauty?

I had a private word, chosen when it occurred to me that Thoder was like Mars himself. I said "old-wise", and found sustaining comfort in the term.

I had begun to move townwards, mechanically, lost in this series of reflections as in opposed mirrors. The thought struck me that here and now I could test one statement of Peter and Lilith's: that they had brought me here unobserved. Did it check? I saw no reason why not. Their penthouse gave direct to mainsurface. There was a beaten track leading away towards the town—the one I was following right now—and it was good enough for wheeled traffic. The rest of the apartment building, of course, was sunk into the side of the rift valley called "canal" millions of miles away and still known by that absurd wet name. There was no convenient point of vantage from which I could look down to see the track between the low levels of town and the base of the apartment block where the main entrance was, but in my weakened state I would not have tackled a long sand-scramble anyhow, so it was vain to regret the lack.

Assume, though, they had spoken truly. I was now retracing the course I had followed, unconscious. In some closed vehicle they could have brought me in secret to the doorway I had passed out of. Check, yes. And the line of this track, from where it lapsed towards the canal floor, bore only ten degrees compass off the direct line to the Old Temple, where they claimed to have found me.

Beyond the Old Temple, my destination, my home, my refuge—and perhaps my teacher.

Peter and Lilith would logically have made inquiries at the spaceport, over there to my left as I approached the setting sun. Learning that a Martian had been in the crew of Lugath's ship, they would have headed next for my own quarter of the city. Their route homeward—yes, it would bring them to the Old Temple. Concede and check.

I felt a little better, even though Thoder would doubtless have warned me not to place too much faith in external evidence. I could almost hear his old croaking voice as he advised, "There are two reasons why a story may be consonant with the observable facts: it may have dictated them, or it may have been dictated by them."

How much more good sense had he taught me, that at the time I dismissed because I was bored, or hankered after the glossy possessions of Earthfolk, Centaurs and Bears? Why had it taken a night of nerve-whipping to show me the value of his teaching?

Because I was a fool.

Peter had said, "You're not a stupid man, according to your trade certificates." But those certificates didn't define the parameters of a man, only of a set of acquired skills.

I came to the tilt of the road, where I could see down the steep slope towards the bottom of the canal. The road, inevitably, hairpinned back and forth. On foot, it was a waste of effort to do the same. I left the beaten solidity of the ground intended for vehicles and trudged straight ahead and downward, with the big familiar strides halfway between a leap and a run made possible by light gravity.

One day they would make gravity cheap enough to do more than pressurise apartments like the one I'd left; already there were such luxuries as nulgee beds, though of course the area affected by the field was comparatively small, and it would cost fantastically to apply the principle to whole buildings. Yet that would probably come sooner or later.

And with it the real crunch. Then, the loyalties would be nakedly exposed. I could stand a few weeks on a world like Durrith, or Goldstar, or Charigol, closer to Earth's gravity and air than Mars was, but I had to walk slowly, conserve energy, eat much more than usual, exercise flat on my back every night to encourage the habit of carrying my own weight; only when I came home did I feel truly able to relax. On Mars my seven feet and four inches stretched out like a growing sandreed; my legs loped down dunesides as now down the canal slope; my small hands, fragile-fingered, could pleat a sandflower petal into a dozen folds before it deliquesced through contact with too great an area of moist skin. (That had been a symbol of delicacy of touch for me since I was three—Mars years. Say five going on six, Earth-style.) Compelled to live permanently under

24

Earthside conditions, I would die of exhaustion before I was middle-aged.

And there were others like me, though as I had thought a little while ago not very many. On the whole planet, as many as a million, in fifteen or twenty towns and settlements.

Of which not one could be called truly Martian. Behind me, I had just left a piece of Earth; it was clearly labelled Grand Canal Apartments, a piece of hollow plaque-service to this foreign world. Lacking Earth-fierce gravity, life in such surroundings would not kill me very quickly, but it would make me deliquesce like a sandflower in an unguarded vase.

Had I been wrong, or stupid, to choose a spaceside career? In some sense, perhaps. There were a high proportion of Martians in spacecrew compared with the population of the home world, that was true, so I had much to excuse my choice. It was a point of honour on certain worlds in Bear space—not including Goldstar, of course—for crewmen's fraternities and other labour organisations to recognise Martian as a nationality, and this had impressed me before I realised it was an ancient human habit to enshrine old prejudices in what had formerly been progressive, liberal, even radical groups. It was plaque-service again, lip-service engraved in metal, and could be traced back to the days when Bears and Centaurs were repeating the decolonisation process familiar from the history of Earth and declaring their independence.

But I'd been genuinely impressed, as also by the idea that the way to make a mark as a Martian was to do something a little dangerous, a little notable. Spacecrewing offered itself. Or one could stay on Mars and *be* a Martian—convincing oneself, possibly, but whom else?

I got the rest of the way to the canal floor without much further thinking; the going was tough, each step sinking my feet deep in finely pulverised sand, and I had to concentrate. Standing on firm ground once more, I glanced left and right. Here, the sun had set long ago, of course, and lights were coming on. Just where the canal bent to disappear from view, the huge gleaming signs of the Centaur Embassy dazzled me—another non-Martian intrusion.

From the same direction a couple of late-running trucks rumbled, still sifting down the dust collected during their traverse of the desert between here and Mariner. (How many more of these ridiculous fossilised terms? "Mariner" on a planet without seas! It had some explanation in terms of pre-space history, but . . .)

I had been intending to go into one of the sidewalks; out here it was shadowy, and inside the big square tunnels there was light. Likewise free air—I checked the pressure meter at the nearest entry lock, recognising the familiar 10 on the dial.

But I hesitated, glancing at the wall of the sidewalk. The upper half, from about waist-height—my waist—was of glass, and meant to be perfectly transparent. This section wasn't. Sand and age and solar radiation had conspired to abrade, discolour and opaque it.

It'll do! This is only Mars, after all!

Shabby things. Worn-out things. Second-best things. That was the status of my home world. And sooner or later . . . full artificial gravity, whether we Martians cared for it or not.

Beyond the half-transparent wall of the sidewalk I saw someone approaching who still had on his mask. I couldn't tell for sure whether it was a Centaur, a Bear or an Earth-sider—indeed, whether it was a man or a woman, for his/her body was thickly wrapped in warm clothes. But someone who couldn't even stand to breathe at pressure ten was a stranger, foreigner, trespasser. I turned quickly away from the sidewalk and began to stride along the road instead, keeping well out of the way of traffic and ensuring that my silhouette was displayed against the sidewalk lighting.

This corner, the one where I'd been left for dead? I bent to stare at the drifted dust close under the embrasure of the Old Temple wall, wondering if the shallow indentation in its upper surface was due to my dumped body, or the result of chance. There was nothing to persuade me one way or the other. Straightening, I surveyed the temple, ground to top, feeling the same curious trembling that had overcome me as a child.

"Temple"? Another Earthside preconception, more than

likely. Yet there was something stately about it, awe-in-spiring even to adopted Martians who could make no better guess at its function than tourists from Earth. It was immense, but plain, like Martian deserts. It rose almost a hundred feet, and had been taller, but along the top edges of its four stone walls time had gnawed rat-fashion, till one could no longer deduce its original height. It had been a lidless box full of sand when it was found. Now, it was emptied, the fifteen inexplicable artifacts discovered during the clearing of the sand were on display in the interior, and visitors came up into it through a tunnel from the sidewalk opposite, to exclaim in disappointment: "Why, it's nothing! *Nah-thing!*"

It might not even have been built by Martians, as such. It might have been made by visitors from another star, when men were grunting in caves. Who cared? It said so much, even roofless and dilapidated. "Look on my works, ye mighty, and despair!"

I considered going inside. At this time of evening it would probably be empty of tourists. And to my shame I'd not been in for years—not, indeed, since before I first shipped into space. The most potent symbol of the uniqueness of Mars in existence, and I'd neglected it.

But I had other urgent errands to perform, someone to find whom I had neglected still worse. I resolved to come back to the Old Temple tomorrow, or at any rate before my next spaceflight.

The resolution was part of the same process of change which had been working in my mind like a ferment—while I was unconscious, perhaps, for it had gone such a long way in a single day. I thought back. Its inception had been when I recalled Thoder's teachings, under the lashing of the nerve-whip. Ever since, I'd been feeling a bubble of fresh awareness expanding in my head, bringing a sort of clarity to my assessment of myself.

Bluntly, I realised as I gazed up at the Old Temple, what I'd done was betray a heritage. I'd dismissed Thoder's sound sense as irrelevant rubbish; I'd preferred four-space analysis and driver theory.

Yet that latter was dealing with machines. Thoder was dealing with men and women. I needed both kinds of learning before I could tackle the task I'd set myself, the discovery of the mystery underlying my last voyage.

I didn't have to wonder which way to take to find Thoder. It was like stepping on to the path which led back to my childhood . . . and beyond that, whither?

V

AT FIRST, whenever I came back to Mars after a long spacetrip, I immediately used to head for this quarter of town, the district where I had spent so much of my youth and acquired what small learning I could lay claim to. Lately I'd lost the habit; now I reflected on the point, it seemed to me I'd grown disheartened with the way things never changed unless for the worse. Pass this way now, and again in a year—the only difference, a door leaning a little more crazily in its frame, another coat of drab paint failing to disguise cracks in cast concrete, the sand-etchings deeper on the glass windows of the sidewalks . . .

There was one minor consolation, though. The people here were Martians. I turned my head to look after a girl who passed. She was only about six foot nine, but she was clearly my kind, my kin, where Lilith—exquisitely and miniaturely beautiful though she might be—was not.

People were mostly in their homes. It was the time of the evening meal. The thought struck me that I should eat too, as I had no way of knowing Thoder's present circumstances, and to have to offer a meal to a returned ex-pupil who arrived without warning after not having eaten since yesterday might be a strain on his purse.

There used to be a restaurant near here . . . I entered the sidewalk by a lock whose pressure meter had a star across the glass of its dial. The lights were on, but no one was to be seen; half-suspecting that the meter's reading of 10 might be a leftover from the time of breakage, I cracked my mask with care. The air was stale, but the pressure was okay. I walked to the next junction, then turned sharply left.

Here, the town edged back into a narrow canyon, a tributary fault of the main canal, and after a hundred yards the two sidewalks merged into a single roofed-over volume.

I'd played Bears and Centaurs up and down the rusty steel pylons supporting that roof when I was five or six. I was amazed to see how badly bowed the pylons had become nowadays. If enough sand had been allowed to drift over the roof to cause that, it must be almost dark by day down here!

Three kids, two boys and a girl already over five feet tall, were playing some foolish game under a thin trickle of sand from a leak. That shocked me further. If the hole was large enough for sand to fall through against the pressure below, it needed to be repaired, and quickly.

Seeing me, they remembered with a start of guilt what they ought to be doing and seized shovels and brooms to clear away the pile of sand, now heaping two feet high.

If no one else has reported that leak, I ought to!

I was too hungry now that I'd started to consider food, though, to take any immediate action. If I recalled aright, the restaurant I was looking for was just around the next curve—

There was *a* restaurant there, its frontage still decorated with old red paint and failing fluorescents, but the name was changed. It had been . . . let me see . . . the Barmecide Feast, a half-sick joke due to some pioneer in the early days of the city, a mocking reference to the scarcity of surplus food-stocks such as might enable a restaurant to offer a proper menu. Those days were a century or more in the past, and one could eat here as well as anywhere, but it was still a shock to see a new name up: Edisu's.

It was a worse shock still to see four Centaur spacemen as the only customers, complaining loudly in their own dialect about the dishes on offer.

I stood for long seconds in the door, half decided to go elsewhere, but then a man whom I took to be the proprietor spotted me and came over with such a pleading look that I accepted his offer of a table. This man was an immigrant from Earth, I judged, a near-pure Negro eighteen inches under my height, still weighed down with Earthside muscles and his big chest still maladjusted to air at pressure 10.

His only waiter was patiently conforming to his title,

standing by until the Centaurs finished showing off with all their grouses and chose their meal.

"What are they doing here?" I demanded of the Negro, on an impulse.

"The—uh—the gentlemen off the Centauran ship?" He swallowed largely, his Adam's apple bobbing up and down. "We see a lot of them around here these days."

"Do you, indeed?" I contemplated the menu. I *had* been away a long time—far longer than I'd realised. I'd moved to a small apartment on the other side of town, to be close to the spaceport, as I imagined, but in truth more because I wanted to escape the nagging sense that I was betraying the heritage.

What there was of it. Neglect, decay, drifted sand on the roof, a broken glass over a pressure meter dial, a new name on a restaurant . . .

"Do you happen to know a man called Thoder?" I asked. "A teacher, who lives around here?"

"I'm afraid not," the Negro said. "I've only been here two years, and—and people are inclined to keep themselves to themselves in this area."

Granted. I chose whipped frozen avocado pulp from Mariner to begin my meal, Sun Lake gravied chicken, and a Phobos salad. The chicken was dressed with some hot spicy African sauce instead of the promised gravy, but the Centaurs had stretched their list of complaints so long I hadn't the heart to register one myself.

Besides, it tasted pretty good in its own right.

I hurried over the meal because I could feel the spurious tiredness due to the nerve-whipping creeping up on me. I'd never been whipped before except by police picking me out of a bar-brawl, and then they confined their attack to putting the arguers into spasm, but I knew that some time tonight —probably within two or three hours—a wave of tiredness would sweep over me like a sandstorm and blot me out. By then I meant to be at home and in bed.

Sensibly, I should go straight there. I wasn't feeling sensible.

It so happened that, despite my eating quickly, the Centaurs concluded their meal a minute before I did, paid their bill and started to gather their gear with loud comments on the standard of Martian food. I thought it best to let them get clear of the place before I left myself, for fear I might be tempted to dispute their views, and that was how I came to see the two Bears arrive: not to eat, but to call for beer and an oware set. The Negro had one, of course. I saw him pick it up from behind the counter, and the pebbles to go with it.

I snapped my fingers to attract his attention. He glanced at the waiting Bears, decided a moment's delay wouldn't harm anyone, and came to me.

"And dice," I said.

"What?" He blinked at me. "They asked for oware, and —"

"So you don't get many Bears in here? Not as many as Centaurs?"

"Why, no. But—"

"Bears gamble. They play oware with the order of moves determined by a round of dice, not in sequence as most people do."

"Ah—thanks for informing me." He gave a sudden weary smile. "I've had enough complaints about the quality of my place's service for one evening."

"You're pro-Bear?"

"Well . . ." He stiffened, warily making sure that the Centaurs were out of earshot. They were; they'd already left the restaurant before the Bears entered, which was as well, or there might have been an exchange of words. "I find them easier customers, to be frank."

"So do I," I admitted.

I waited till he had delivered oware and dice to them, thinking how, until my recent experience in Centaur space, I'd clung dogmatically to the principle that no Martian should take sides between Centaur and Bear, especially not to copy the standard Earthside prejudice; how I'd assigned my own preponderant preference for working in Bear space to the Bears' own greater willingness to hire Old System crewmen. It was doubtless true that all human beings were human, but how they behaved made a hell of a lot of difference. Bears tended to be happy-go-lucky, individualistic, great improvisers, and keen gamblers. Centaurs were formal, disciplined, great organisers, and used even their leisure time to improve themselves, studying or engaging in elaborate well-analysed games designed to encourage intellection.

I wondered what Centaur girls were like in bed. While on Durrith I'd had neither the spare time nor the spare funds to find out.

When I emerged on to the sidewalk, the Centaurs were nowhere to be seen. Grateful for that, I headed in the direction of Thoder's place, the shadows of youth closing around me, memories springing from every house and open space I passed. Lost in musing reminiscence, I was startled to be shouted at less than a quarter-mile from my goal.

"Hey, you there!"

The same four Centaurs I'd seen in the restaurant were gathered in an uncertain knot ahead of me. Their rank-insignia labelled them as a junior purser, two spacehands and an air technician: low on the Centaur totempole. It could have been worse. I'd found the officers intolerable, but some of the lower grades were willing to accept Old Systemers as equals.

It was the purser who'd addressed me. He held a slip of card with some scribbled writing on it—probably an address they were trying to find. My guess was confirmed on his next words.

"Do you know this district? We can't find this place we want to get to."

"I was raised here," I said shortly, and approached them. The air technician, who was what one would call short even by Earthside standards, blinked up at me shyly and displayed un-Centaur-like awe at my seven-four. Stupid! With one-gee muscle on him, he could have broken an arm off me like the wing of a chicken.

"Let me see," I said, and took the card. Reading it, I had the greatest shock of this shock-filled evening.

I knew that address better than my own name. But what in the entire Galaxy would four lowly Centaur spacemen want at the home of an obscure Martian teacher, rejected even by some of his old pupils?

I covered my astonishment and gave the card back with a nod. "As it happens, I'm going that way," I said.

I didn't speak an offer to guide them; they didn't utter

thanks for guidance. Silent, we trudged the last few hundred yards, while my mind spun busily, random as a roulette-wheel.

The possible explanations I threw up didn't include the true one. It took confrontation with my goal to enlighten me, and when I saw it, I felt a pang of nausea.

Thoder was no longer where he had been. There were new garish signs on the old house I'd known so well: transparent plaques in the shape of escutcheons, on to which were projected from behind coloured representations of famous arms. I'd never taken much stock of heraldry myself, but before venturing into Centaur space I'd had to pick up enough of the rudiments to blazon all the commoner devices, as Centaurs took the whole business very seriously. Party per pale, first a field sable semé of stars and comets argent, second vert a tiger's head erased proper gardant— that was the Tyrant of Centaurus's own bearing, obviously a come-on for the promising clients. It faded, and was replaced by another I didn't recognise, probably a recent invention: quarterly battled-embattled azure and argent.

Around me the Centaurs began to chatter. As always, they hated to be at a loss, for it made them feel vaguely inferior. Now they were in sight of where they were going, they resumed their customary affectation of arrogance.

They strode towards the door flanked by the escutcheons, and I trailed after them unwillingly until I was close enough to read the signboard between the dazzling lights. It said: *MARTIAN COLLEGE OF HERALDS—Zond King of Arms.*

An awful possibility occurred to me. This "King of Arms" . . . could it actually *be* Thoder? Deserted by so many of his pupils, as I had deserted him, driven at last to this mockery of learning, this arid study of pretentious ancestries?

Let it not be so!

The door opened, revealing a fawning stranger who practically hunched forward in his attempt to avoid dominating the "distinguished patrons" with his Martian stature. He was seven-six at least. It shamed me to see him struggling to disguise that noble tallness. I hesitated until the Centaurs had gone inside, waited yet a moment or two longer, then in my turn strode over to bang on the door.

VI

"THODER?" the man said sharply, studying me with keen attention. "No, he hasn't been here for a long time now. Who are you, anyway?"

He wasn't stooping for me, which was a marked improvement. To encourage continued verticality I was making the most of my own height.

Before answering, I made a quick survey of the vestibule where we were standing. It was dizzily disorienting to recognise familiar shapes, familiar items of furniture, among the superficial differences: the artificially faded facsimiles of ancient Earthside arms, the stacked piles of various *Journals of Genealogy*, outwardly gaudy with colourful devices and inwardly mock-scientific with their pokerfaced analyses of complicated family relationships.

In a room over to the left I could hear the Centaurs' voices. Typically, though they had been here literally three minutes, they were already complaining of being kept waiting.

I said at length, "I'm a former pupil of his. I—ah—I wanted to look him up, that's all. He's still alive, isn't he?"

Somehow I'd never considered the chance of his having died in the long interim, but now, surrounded by visible testimony of the passage of time, I felt the idea real and oppressive.

"What is it, Yuma?"

The interruption came from a brisk woman—Martian, stately without being at all beautiful—who had emerged from a room on the right. She wore a curious long coat hanging in straight panels to below her knees, striped in the full range of heraldic colours even to being trimmed with vair and counter-vair at the cuffs of the sleeves, ermine and counter-ermine at the hem.

"An inquiry for Thoder," the man said. "He's a former disciple, he says."

Disciple? An odd word. Thoder had never termed his students anything but "pupil". But I had no time to think about that—the woman had immediately confronted me.

34

"I can probably tell you where to find him," she said after a scrutiny of my appearance that seemed to satisfy her. "Is it a long time since you saw him, though? Yes, it must be, or you'd not have come to this house."

"Why do you ask?" I parried.

"No special reason—merely that he's retired from active work and I hear he's . . ."

"Sick?"

"I don't believe so. Just retired, and turned his attention to other matters. What's your name?"

I hesitated. "Ray Mallin," I said at length, not finding any rational grounds for withholding it.

The woman glanced at Yuma, who closed his eyes briefly as if examining an imaginary list. He said rapidly, "That's a sound Martian familial! Ah—four, five, *six* generations native. Last Earthside branch-in was the great-great-grandmother paternal-lateral right. Hmmm . . . Interesting!" He regarded me with patent curiosity.

His curiosity was nothing to my astonishment. Despite my habitual disapproval of heraldry, I was shaken to hear this complete stranger displaying a knowledge of my descent more exact than my own. I said, "How do you know that? I've never had my genealogy traced!"

"Yuma is an eidetic," the woman said. "An invaluable skill in our profession. Presumably you have cousins or some other relatives elsewhere, who've consulted us." She gave Yuma an inquiring glance.

"That's odd," the eidetic said with a frown. "I hadn't thought of it before, but . . ." He bit his lip. "Normally I wouldn't carry cousin-degree data so close to the top of my mind, so—oh, of course!" His expression lightened. "It was only a couple of days ago that somebody was making inquiries about the Mallin strain."

Little warning lights began to flash inside my skull. I said in a carefully controlled voice, "Really? One of these —ah—cousins from elsewhere, perhaps?"

"Precisely. A Centaur officer, a certain Major Housk, from Leovang." Yuma was nodding repeatedly as if pleased with the accuracy of his recollection. "We gave him an extremely detailed list of the collaterals. No doubt he'll be trying get in touch with you. He was particularly eager to track down the Mallins."

I was dreadfully tired—the aftermath of the nerve-whipping catching up with me—but that didn't prevent me seeing a high-order probability under my nose: that this Centaur major had *already* been in touch with me. Last night.

"Fascinating," I said with all the warmth I could muster. "I begin to see why people enthuse about heraldry these days when it can be the means of reuniting far-flung branches of one's family. Did you by any chance learn where Major Housk is staying? Perhaps I could contact him."

"I'm afraid he didn't say," Yuma shrugged.

Too bad. Still, at least I had one valid clue to be going on with.

The Centaurs in the other room were beginning to get noisy. Yuma caught the woman's attention and jerked his head towards the source of the row. She sighed and returned to my original inquiry.

"Thoder's current address . . . Yuma can give it to you. If you'll excuse me, I must attend to my clients."

"Are *you* 'Zond King of Arms'?" I demanded.

"Why not? Would you expect me to be called 'queen'?" She gave a curious twisted smile. "A most un-heraldic term, my friend! Like a chairman, a King of Arms is a King regardless of physical gender."

That way led to another of Thoder's favourite precepts: the term is not the thing named. And abruptly I was in a hurry to be gone and continue my search.

The address Yuma gave me took me aback. I had a vague recollection of the district in which it lay, more than a mile distant. It was an area I preferred to avoid, being much favoured by offworld visitors and having accordingly the majority of its sidewalks pressurised to six or five . . . An irritating insight struck me: I resented that at least partly because tolerant or not people of other planets tended to regard me as a freak for my tallness, and it was good to be at home while they were struggling for breath.

Not that a pressure of 10 ought to inconvenience Earthsiders, really. Allegedly, primitive mountain-climbers had reached twenty (some said twenty-five) without artificial aids, and whole communities existed as high as twelve, in the Andes where some of my own ancestors hailed from.

I reviewed the layout of the city in my mind. I would have to continue from here by cab; time was running short, my tiredness was growing, and I needed a clear mind to talk to Thoder.

I paused automatically at the pressuriser adjacent to the sidewalk lock I first came to, fumbling for coins to pay for the recharge of my mask. I'd worn the mask a lot since coming away from Grand Canal Apartments because of that irrational impulse to stay on the open street instead of going into the sidewalk. But Peter and Lilith had been generous when they had it serviced. Seeing that I'd used barely a quarter of the reservoir, I decided I could recharge it later.

I used more, trudging in search of a cab, but I finally spotted one and instructed it to take me to Thoder's.

Folded awkwardly on the padded seat, I wondered about my mysterious Centaur "relative". Perhaps it hadn't struck Yuma and his employer that it was strange a man should ask about kinfolk whose closest possible link was five generations past. No, why should it? Centaurs were like that. I remembered the Chief Officer who'd dumped me on Durrith, with his vaunted "family connection" linking him to the Tyrant himself. I didn't know how close the relationship was, but it certainly couldn't have been very direct, or he'd have been at least captain rather than Chief.

Housk? Did that name mean anything to me? Of course not. I'd never been a heraldry bug, and I probably couldn't even have remembered the birthname of my mother's mother. She hadn't been around to tell me.

Nor, come to that, had my mother. She'd died bearing me. It still could happen. And my father was a sad tired old man around the planet in somewhere like Voyager, or perhaps by this time he'd moved on again ...

I didn't like thinking about my family much. What there was of it. Thoder had been half a father to me as well as a teacher, and my natural father had been glad to leave me to his care.

Customarily I would think of my isolation as a form of self-sufficiency, a really Martian pattern of behaviour. Le-

gally Earth citizens, we were in a sense rejected by everyone; why not suit deeds to circumstances and accept lone-
liness?

I was beginning to discover why not.

In any case, I told myself as I resumed my earlier train
of thought, Housk might well not be the man's own name.
It could have been borrowed to lend plausibility to his inquiry after a member of the Mallin strain. If it was genuine, then I'd learned something surprising about my own
background. Though on principle I'd not have admitted it,
I'd have expected my collateral forebears to have opted
for Bear space rather than Centaur.

For this assumption I had no grounds whatever, I now
realised. The typus of Bear and Centaur must have evolved
over several generations, only recently becoming so sharply
defined that one could make blanket statements of the
kind, "Centaurs are rigid and authoritarian, Bears informal
and given to gambling."

Yet for all this, I retained the obscure feeling that the
roots of the archetypes must go deep: as though from the
very earliest days of interstellar colonisation one character
had looked towards Ursa Major, the other towards Centaurus.
Long before the succession of economic disasters which had
caused them to revive the ancient institution of a "tyrant"—
a dictator *pro tem.* until the crisis passed—and then to
organise their lives on a permanent impending-catastrophe
basis, the Centaurs must have foreshadowed in little their
present condition. So too with the Bears, although their
random habits and lack of system made it hard to pin down
exact starting-points for any change.

I suddenly found myself thinking of a girl I'd known
on Charigol. I'd come halfway to falling in love with her,
the only time I ever considered marrying and raising
children anywhere but on Mars. I wondered if that was
why I'd pictured my ancestors heading Ursawards.

Better for me to have been born generations earlier, at
the time when—as Yuma had put it—the last non-native
"branch-in" occurred in my family. In those days, there
was no question of independent power-blocs enclosing the
Old System; the colonies were quasi-federal dependent states,
the first seeds of Martian pride, Martian traditions and Mar-

tian physique were sprouting excitingly. In my time, in this depressing modern age, it seemed to me that Old System was roofed-in against the sands of space, and there were leaks.

My head spun. I was almost worn out, sleep dragging at my eyelids like Earth-normal gravity, intolerably heavy. But I concentrated on the idea of seeing Thoder again. I must say to him something of these confusing new ideas plaguing me, ask his opinion and guidance about them . . .

Getting very close now. The cab nosed to the sidewalk lock nearest to the actual address. I masked up for the few paces I'd have to go to reach it, slid payment into the fare slot, and unfolded myself out of the vehicle. Yet one more irritation! Why did these things have to be scaled to dwarfs of a mere six-six or so?

Because the people on Mars who mostly used cabs were from higher-gravity worlds like Earth. Damn them.

I blinked at the façade of my destination. I was glad to see that in moving away from strictly Martian surroundings Thoder had apparently gone up the ladder of prosperity several rungs. This house was kept in good order, freshly painted and carefully repaired. I only hoped that to secure this well-earned benefit in his retirement he hadn't had to betray his Martian principles.

So much, so *much* had changed! And I'd been too wrapped up in my own selfish affairs to notice what was going on.

VII

BUT THODER hadn't changed. Oh, outwardly yes—the lean frame more stooped, the white hair thinner, the eyes buried more deeply in a close net of wrinkles. Inwardly, where it counts, he hadn't altered a jot.

I'd planned a long apology by way of introduction, and it was unnecessary. He recognised me, greeted me as if I'd left him days ago rather than years, made me welcome and seated me in a large, cluttered room like a cross-section of a lifetime. Diagrams, charts and racked bookspools lined the walls; every available shelf or flat surface bore items such as he had used to teach unwilling me and my companions the elements of life-knowledge, picked up or given to him as gifts. Beads on strings struck a familiar chord in my memory, but there were new objects I didn't recognise, a good few of them imported by the look of them: Tibetan prayer-wheels, a group of Bear statuettes representing Apprehension, Hope and Certainty, a Centaur game-board of a type I'd seen in use on Durrith but lacked the lifetime habituation needed to play upon . . .

Thoder wasn't a schoolteacher, of course. I'd had the regular schooling of any Martian child, or else I'd never have been able to qualify in four-space engineering. He was more—well, I'd heard some of his adult admirers call him a guru, and once I'd sneaked a look at the definition of that term in his dictionary. I'd already been of an age to be self-assertive and cocky, so I felt it demeaning to have to ask him directly for an explanation of the word. I'd found something like: "An instructor in spiritual values, especially in the precepts of ancient Indian mystical teachings."

I'd never heard of a starship being driven by prayer-wheels, so that information had also reinforced my intention of breaking with Thoder and shipping out to the stars.

It wasn't that I didn't *like* the guy. I—you might say I loved him, because he was closer to me than my father had been during my later childhood. It was simply that, for all the analogies he could draw between the stark Martian landscape and the formation of a truly Martian personality, I regarded his precepts as irrelevant to modern times. He spoke in terms of the individual; I looked at the news of the great power-blocs, numbering scores of planetary systems and billions of people. He spoke of fulfilment as a Martian; I thought of the legalistic gesture of contempt implied by my being officially an Earthside citizen, even though I would die young if I had to spend my life on my so-called "home" world. And I drifted off.

He brought me refreshment—little nutty biscuits, cups of local coffee—and seated himself with slow care in a large chair facing me.

"You look very tired," he said abruptly.

"Well . . ." I sought a tactful way to phrase the reason for my visit. With characteristic sharpness, he slashed aside the veils of prevarication.

"Ray! I know, I don't have to be told, that only some extraordinary event would bring you back to me! I'd guess that something had happened to you which has made you see that a fuller understanding of what I used to try and drive through your armoured pate might guide you to a solution of—of whatever problem confronts you. If that's so, then I don't need apologies or excuses. I planted a seed of awareness in you, and now it's blooming. What more reward should a man ask?"

"I'm sorry," I muttered. "It was a kind of insult to think otherwise." I sipped the coffee he had given me. "What's happened, as briefly as I can summarise it, is—"

I told him about the four men in privacy screens who had waylaid me last night as I wandered through the canal-floor city. I told him what they had demanded of me, how I had failed to tell them what they wanted to know, how I had been rescued on the verge of dust-drowning by two strangers from Earth, how my quest for him had led me to the woman who called herself Zond King of Arms and how her assistant Yuma had unwittingly given me a clue to my assailants in the shape of a name which might or might not be genuine, that of Major Housk the Centaur officer.

He listened with utter attention, scarcely moving except to take his long slow chest-filling Martian breaths. When I came to the end of my story, he was silent for the space of three further breaths—I counted them—and then drew himself back to the present from whatever reach of extended time he had retired to in order to re-examine my tale.

He said, "Give me more details of the voyage. The name of the ship?"

"The *Hippodamia*."

He rubbed his chin. "Do you know what that means?"

I started. "No! Is it significant?"

"Is it—? Ray, I'd thought that you paid more heed to my instruction than *that*. At least you can't have forgotten the origin of the term Centaur?"

I frowned. Tiredness was gnawing at the foundations of my consciousness, eroding it like a sandbank before the wind. "A race in ancient mythology, half horse, half human, supposed to have been an ignorant primitive tribe's impression of their first contact with men riding horseback."

"A gross oversimplification, but let it suffice. *Hippodamia* means 'tamer of horses'—hence by association tamer of Centaurs. There is much to be learned regarding the process of human intellection from studying ancient lore, Ray; it enshrines what people themselves thought worth singling out from their day-to-day experience in an age before the advent of psychology and scientific self-analysis."

He gave me a searching stare. "Would you rather I delayed this—this attempt to sort out your muddled information? There is far more of it available to you than you seem to realise, but perhaps it's only your exhaustion hampering you. Tomorrow you may arrive at the right answers yourself."

"No, please." I blinked away the weight of sleep on my eyelids. "I do need your help, and quickly too."

"Hah! In the state you're in, how much of it will you absorb? I speak in riddles, or so you once accused me—still, let the past lie where it falls. I'll go on for a short while, at least."

His eyes shifted to focus blankly beyond the wall at my back.

"You maintain you spent the entire voyage attending to excessively powerful engines, likely to separate themselves from the hull if they weren't continually supervised. But you must have made the acquaintance of your colleagues?"

"Half of them I never knew by name. I ate and slept in the driver compartment."

"What was the purpose of the ship's voyage?"

"Purpose? Why—ah—she was carrying cargo, and about a dozen or so passengers, none of whom I met. I didn't inquire. I'd been soured on travel under Centaur command during my trip to Durrith. Coming back, I was satisfied that I was on the way home, and the fact that Captain Lugath was easier to serve under than any other Centaur I'd ever run across was a kind of bonus."

"It sounds as though you let your mind be turned off by unpleasant experience, instead of profiting from it."

"It's all very well to sit here on Mars and preach!" I snapped. "You hadn't been stranded on a high-gravity world for weeks and weeks, afraid you'd have to come back DTS and lose a year of your life in service to a foreign government!"

"It can't have been all that unbearable," Thoder murmured, "or you'd have gambled an intolerable now against an indefinable future."

I hadn't meant to snap at him. I mumbled an apology. He took no notice.

"Speaking of gambling and 'un-Bear-able', that reminds me. Did you know that bears, apart from man's closest relatives among Earthside fauna such as apes, are the only creatures we've ever discovered with a sense of humour well enough developed to allow them to play jokes on each other? And did you also know that the most disciplined body of men in all our history were the horsemen of the Mongol Khans, who said, 'Our home is on horseback', and lived in the saddle for days together, not even descending to answer Nature's call?"

I couldn't fathom the relevance of that. He waited to be sure I was floundering, then chuckled.

"Speaking in riddles again, am I? Well, back to the subject. What *else* did you think was unusual about Captain Lugath?"

I tensed. This was more like the Thoder I recalled! I'd said nothing about the inspiration that had come to me when I was leaving Peter and Lilith—my moment of insight into Lugath's reaction when I heedlessly asked if his ship was bound direct for Earth, which I'd glossed as suggesting that he was not in fact Centaur, but an Earthman, and afraid his pose had been penetrated. Now I revealed this, and Thoder nodded.

"Do you begin to accept that you really have far more data than you can currently organise into a pattern? Insights like these lead to more and more comprehension."

I had the absurd feeling that he was stalling. The idea seemed to have come to me from nowhere. I held my breath and tried to perform another of the actions he had long ago shown me: reviewing the steps by which the present had been reached to determine any overlooked turning-point.

Had he not shifted the direction of his gaze for a moment, a minute or two ago? I glanced around to see what he might have been looking at, and saw only a wall-chronometer in the area he'd scanned. That couldn't make him deliberately elusive, surely. Say—oh, say he was expecting a visitor at some early time; he'd be direct enough to tell me, "Ray, you come without warning, and I have an appointment. Forgive me, but you must return tomorrow."

I said, "Thoder, I'd always rather take a direct path than a roundabout one. I had time to examine my captors of last night. Despite their privacy screens and disguised voices, I must have observed many things which could help me to identify them. You used to teach that pain was a keen reinforcement of learning to all aware beings—I had pain enough to last me for life in the space of a few hours. I want you to help me recover in detail all the things I saw, heard, smelt and felt while they were questioning me."

He breathed twice while debating how to reply. At last he shrugged.

"Ray, in your present condition you'd lose what you learned almost at once. Go home. Rest. Come back to me when you're recovered, and we'll consider your suggestion."

"No!" I was on my feet without realising I'd moved. "By tomorrow—even, possibly, by now—they may be aboard a Centaur spaceship and out of reach for good!"

"If I told you here and now that they were on their way to the port to make their escape, you couldn't do anything to prevent it. Be reasonable, boy!" He also was creaking off his chair. "Do as I say and go home to rest."

"You're trying to get rid of me," I accused. "Why?"

"Someone is coming to see me," he said. "He's due at any moment."

"But he's not yet here," I pointed out. "I came to call on you without notice, I grant that, but I remember what you used to say when someone was late for a study appointment, in the days when I was a pupil of yours too. You'd always refuse to sit simply waiting, saying it was foolish to waste a gift of time!"

I was now on the verge of passing out from the consequences of my whipping, and but for my impression that he was not being open with me, I'd have accepted his orders to go and rest. As it was, I was desperate to get to the bottom of this petty mystery.

Before he could contrive a persuasive reply, however, a figure passed across the window beside me, the one looking direct on to the sidewalk, and I jolted my head around in time to recognise who it was. For seconds I refused to frame the name to myself; not till the sound of knocking at the door made the association inescapable did I let myself think, "His visitor—it's Lugath! It's Lugath of all the billions in the galaxy!"

That was too much for me. I had a wild picture of a conspiracy enclosing me, of cages barring me in, of traps in an innocent-looking pathway into which I was about to fall. The shock weakened my grip on awareness, and I toppled into the void of darkness which had been threatening to engulf me these past three hours.

Thoder ...
Lugath ...
Sense of humour ... the most disciplined body of ...
Nothing.

VIII

BEFORE OPENING my eyes, I stretched luxuriously with all my joints cracking, thinking how wonderful it was to be back in my own bed, scaled to my length of limb. On how many worlds, aboard how many ships between those worlds, had I had to make do with the hammock I carried rolled in with my regular duffel, because there wasn't a bed to be had on which I could get a night's sleep without waking cramped and stiff?

And the comfort of nulgee flotation—

The intrusion of that thought startled me. I blinked fully awake, momentarily imagining that I wouldn't see what I expected to see: the bedroom of my tiny apartment close to the spaceport.

Yes, the surroundings were absolutely familiar. In which case—why that ridiculous fleeting notion that I owned a nulgee bed? Even if I'd been able to afford one on which a seven foot four inch sleeper could enjoy his rest, the last place I'd want to put it would be here on my home planet. Martian gravity was light, and suited me fine. If

I went to Earth I'd not only want one, I'd have to get one—

For the second time, I brought my mind up short with all forward jets. Go to Earth? Go to *Earth?* I never intended in my whole life to go there! I could picture myself among Earthside crowds, a hunched, gangling, awkward giant, a figure of fun, a spectacle for children to gawk at. On Earthside worlds in other systems I'd experienced a faint shadow of such treatment, but the rigidity of Centaur upbringing and the stress they laid on disciplined politeness prevented open mockery even by children, while there was always an undertone of friendliness in Bears which mitigated the impact—one could tell there was no malice in the most unconcealed amusement.

A dream, possibly, was responsible for these misplaced notions. I frowned, worrying backwards into the vacuum of sleep, and convinced myself that I'd been dreaming about real events in my past life. For example, it wouldn't be surprising if my subconscious interpreted my forced stay on Durrith, prisoner of circumstances and unable to escape from the tiring drag of extra weight, as a sort of physical analogue to my resentment of being legally an Earth citizen. And I'd been in a nulgee bed, rare though such things were except on that decadently luxurious planet I had no wish to visit. On Charigol, wasn't it? Yes, there'd been this Bear girl—tall for her kind, which was why I'd picked her out.

"Of course she was tall!" I said aloud, suddenly frightened for no apparent reason.

My mind had delivered me a picture of her as *tiny*.

Well, not exactly a picture. A compound of sense-impressions combining the recollection of her face upturned to mine from a long way below, plus a feeling of having to bend right down to be close, plus the ever-present tug of gravity which she didn't feel . . .

No, of course she was tall, that girl with whom I'd shared a nulgee bed. Determined to prove it, I leaned across to the drawer of the storage unit in which I tossed odds and ends, like souvenirs of people I never expected to see again.

My eye was caught, as I turned, by the chronometer on the bedside locker. It showed a few minutes before noon.

If I'd slept *that* long, no wonder my mind was muzzy. I was almost always up by an hour after dawn when I was

home on Mars; only the weariness of fighting a high-gee
planet could knock me out for a morning as well as a night.
By reflex I checked the other dialled instruments standing
there—pressure meter steady at 10, humidity meter up
a little, temperature around 21°, on the warm side.

I'd been sweating in my sleep. The fact had only just
occurred to me. The sheet in which I was wrapped was a
trifle clammy. With the heat high, the humidity likewise, that
was nothing too remarkable. Yet there was also this mental
confusion . . . Fever?

The sensible thing was to check myself right away and
make sure I hadn't picked up a virus. But the nagging impression of the nulgee bed, which I couldn't account for,
refused to let me do the sensible thing. I had to locate
a particular solido cube in among my junk, and verify the
question about this girl on Charigol. She *had* been tall, I
was absolutely sure: not Mars-tall, naturally, but exceptional
for her kind, something like six-five, with golden skin, black
hair, a touch of almond about the eyes. Very attractive.
And I'd had a solido taken of us that afternoon during car-
nival week, by the garden entrance of the house where they
rented out nulgee beds to merrymakers— Ah, there: the shiny
upper side of a solido cube glinting among a miscellany
of rubbish. I took it out and felt a moment of total dissociation.

She was tall, all right; we were standing side by side
on level ground, with my arm draped around her shoulder.
But she wasn't black-haired, gold-skinned, almond-eyed.
She was a dark-blonde Scand with one-eighth Watussi responsible for her extra inches, her brown eyes and the faint
cocoa-dusting of her skin.

For long seconds I stared disbelievingly at the solido.
Then I hurled it violently back in the drawer and strode
to the bath cabinet. Bath—another Earthside term like "canal"
and the name of the town Mariner. Martians had better uses
for water in multi-gallon quantities than heating it, lounging
in it and throwing it away. Sprays of airborne detergent
were much more efficient at both cleansing and deodorising.
Also they didn't involve the extra fuss of having to get dry
afterwards, whether with towels that expended clothing-
quality fibre or air-ducts that took up excessive room.

I had a good range of medical preparations and devices in here. Travelling to so many different worlds, and dependent for continued employment on a clean health-certificate, all spacemen got into the habit of watching their immunities. I gave myself the most thorough working-over I'd ever attempted, marked up my emergencies—only Scale K diagnosis card, and set it against the back-lighted screen of the reader.

Symptoms: sweating in the night, oversleeping, irrational perceptions, confusion of memory. I'd added tension, not knowing if this was natural reaction to discovering my condition, or whether it was part of a syndrome.

Diagnoses possible: Larchman's disease, Group III fevers, combination of mental disorder (NOT FOR SELF-MEDICATION!), with a Group II fever, shock reaction in certain personality-types. A reassuringly short list. Scale K cards were up to hospital standard; the next thing beyond involved computers.

The possibility of Larchman's disease worried me. Contraction of it meant automatic quarantine and a therapy lasting three months if you were lucky. I soaked the appropriate reaction-wafer in saliva and waited half a minute to see if it turned green.

It stayed white.

Fevers? None that I had tests for, anyway. My body-temperature was about .15 of a degree above my usual waking level, but the day was far advanced and I was probably into the first swing of my evening cyclic rise.

Shock reaction in certain types . . . I scanned the list and located myself in the second sub-section.

What kind of shock could I possibly have had that so upset my normal calm mind? I struggled to recall the events of last evening. I'd gone out on the town—I'd eaten in a small restaurant where there were some Centaurs, or possibly Bears . . .

Worse than ever! I couldn't confuse a Centaur and a Bear on the dark side of Pluto! Yet here I was unable to decide which had been in the restaurant at the same time as I was.

Both? The idea seemed reasonable; I accepted it because I had no better alternative, and worked my foggy way forward.

Because of finding so many offworlders in what I'd thought of as being a mainly Martian district, I'd decided to do something which as a Martian I ought to do pretty often, but had neglected for years. I'd gone to the Old Temple to look around.

Then there was something about my ancestry, and the so-called "science" of heraldry. I could understand feeling an access of pride at my purely Martian extraction—it fitted my usual patterns of thinking, and moreover there weren't all that many families which had been native for six generations. Some, the heralds said, went back for twelve or more, but I'd always thought heraldry was a lot of spacedust—

I put my hands to my temples. Where was all this leading me? To a psychiatrist, for urgent treatment? There were two completely contradictory concepts fighting to dominate my mind: one, the familiar dismissal of heraldry as nonsense, and two, the sense that there must be something vital in it, coloured by this pride in my ancestry.

I steadied my mind by degrees. Back to Square One. I'd been out on the town, I'd gone to the Old Temple, I'd . . .

No use. I slapped my hands on my thighs and went to get dressed and order breakfast. There was only one conclusion that fitted the facts: someone had slipped me a Finn. For what purpose, I couldn't imagine. Dressing, I satisfied myself that all my belongings were where they ought to be, including the only item of real value to a robber, my engineer's papers.

Funny. It still didn't explain how I got home, though it did suggest a reason why I'd slept so long. But the drug must have worked its way out of my system by now. I'd passed water before I thought of saving some to test for excreted traces, and what I could squeeze out following my breakfast tested neutral.

Problems on this level, though, worried me so little it was as though I'd taken a tranquilliser. And gradually the disturbance to which I'd woken dissipated. I was satisfied to accept that someone had given me knockout drops, I'd suffered the aftermath of them as I was waking, and now I was all right. Today . . . Today, I decided, it might be interesting to go to the Old Temple again, and this time look the whole place over, study the fifteen famous artefacts on display there, refresh my stale memory of them. After all, they were chief among the unique things about Mars.

I went down to bottom-level of the apartment block and crossed the foyer to check the mail-rack. I found one item addressed to me, one of my father's sad rambling letters containing the usual half-hearted invitation to come around the planet and see him next time I was stopping over. He was in Pegasus now, not Voyager, but he didn't explain why he'd moved on. He was always moving on, as though stepping through a pathetic shadow-copy of my own roamings.

Perhaps that was why, as the years slipped away, we got on together less and less well. Perhaps he was jealous of my qualifications and achievements. He was what Martians called a jobbing-man: a general maintenance technician and handyman, occasionally hiring out as a mere labourer.

Of course, we could do with more maintenance. There was a leak in the roof which I'd seen . . .

Where? I started. Where had I been, that I'd seen a leaky roof sifting down sand?

A misplaced childhood memory, I decided, forced to the surface as part of my unusually vivid dream of last night—this morning, rather. For I could clearly picture three kids playing around in the drizzle of dust.

"Ray!"

No, this simply wasn't good enough. I—

"Ray!" Wheezing up to me came shrivelled old Gus Quaison, manager of this block. He was an Earth immigrant, but a nice enough guy after twenty-five years here. I set aside my preoccupation and greeted him.

"There was someone asking for you this morning," he said. "A Centaur officer, name of Major Housk. Un . . ."

"Centaur?" I said feelingly. "Gus, my last trip was into Centaur space. I hadn't shipped far in that direction before, and never on a Centaur vessel. And after that—well, let's say that if I never see another Centaur it'll be too soon."

"Thought you might feel that way," Gus chuckled. "I've heard you let your hair down about them once or twice before, haven't I? Though you were always neutral on principle between them and the Bears. I told him you were out, anyway, and he left an address for you to contact him. Want it?"

"Did he say what for?" I was puzzled.

"No." Gus's sharp eyes scanned my face. "You don't know him, huh?"

"Housk? I don't think so. And if he's a major I doubt if I want to."

Gus grinned and made to move off. I checked him with a gesture. "Say, there's one thing! How did I get home last night?"

"Don't you know? What did you do, drink youself under?" When I didn't give a better answer than a scowl, he shrugged. "*I'm* supposed to know? I wasn't here, was I? I go off duty at sundown, and you weren't back by then. I thought you'd picked up a girl and were staying over with her again."

IX

THE SIGNIFICANCE of that last little word "again" only hit me when I happened to glance, several minutes later and a good distance away, at the dial of a datime clock.

I was briefly giddy, thinking of the stale pointless joke about the wallowers on Goldstar, fat beasts almost hidden in liquid mud, moving from their wallows once a year at mating-season.

"What day is it?" one wallower asks another.

Pause of several hours. "Tuesday."

Pause, longer still. "Funny! I keep thinking it's Wednesday . . ."

And Gus had said, "Stay over with her *again*."

Almost anywhere else I'd been, bar Durrith, I'd have been inclined to accept the possibility of a two-day binge. I'd have spent half of it sleeping where I'd fallen, owing to the strain of carrying my own weight in a one-gee environment. I was in the habit of preparing for such an eventuality: never carrying more money than I could afford to have stolen while I was dead to the galaxy, for instance. And in most of the pleasure-quarters of most worlds in Bear space, the time of day mattered scarcely at all.

But on Mars you didn't do that. There weren't the resources here to support such binges—a source of complaint among visiting spacemen.

Especially on Mars I as a Martian didn't do that. I felt it was out of place, though being a native I could probably have organised things better than a stranger. I liked to be at home, where I could forget about precautions like carrying a minimum of money. No Martian would rob an unconscious man; at least, I didn't want to have proof that this proud declaration wasn't true, or even be forced into the suspicion that it wasn't thanks to some dirty offworlder not bred to Martian standards of honour.

Then . . . where had I been, what had I done, after going out on the town the night before last?

Not last night; the night before.

I stopped in my tracks, turned aside to the nearest bar I spotted, and sat, sweating for a much better reason than too-high heat and humidity in my apartment. Someone slipping me a Finn was too pat an explanation, especially as it failed to jibe with my retaining all the things a robber would be apt to take. I put the tips of my fingers on the flat wad of papers in my innermost pocket, confirming by touch that I hadn't lost anything.

I found a stylo and drew up a list of what I'd salvaged from whatever wreck my memory had suffered. When I'd completed it, I was none the wiser. What could there be in common between the Old Temple, a girl with almond eyes and golden skin, and a nulgee bed? What could have muddled Bears with Centaurs for me? Where had I been when I saw a drizzle of sand leaking through an ill-maintained section of roof?

I hesitated over the last item and finally struck it out. Three children playing suggested too strongly that this was a dream-image from my youth.

I had one possible inroad on this mystery. Gus had said that a Major Housk was after me, a Centaur, and he'd left an address at which I could contact him. I hadn't taken that address. I was a fool. Should I go back and collect it?

It seemed a reasonable idea. Whether or not Centaurs had

such thin skin they would harbour a grudge indefinitely, it was strange to hear that one of them wanted to contact me, and the only explanation I could think of was that the Chief Officer I'd been rude to actually exercised some influence thanks to his boasted family connection with the Tyrant, and had sent someone to complete the settlement of accounts.

Which still left most of what I knew shrouded in mist. I didn't really believe my own conclusions; I simply had nothing better.

Minutes later, Gus was blinking at me in embarrassment. He said, "Ray, you told me you didn't want anything to do with the guy! So I put the card in the disposall!"

"Oh, for—!" I caught myself. No use swearing at Gus. He was quite right—I had insisted I didn't want to meet any Centaur majors. "Can you remember any details of the address?"

"What's come over you?" he demanded. "Just now you were wishing all Centaurs to the Coalsack, and now you're —"

"Gus!" I blasted. He flinched and put on a frown.

"There was a comweb number with it, I do remember that. Ah—it had a double-five in it."

"Is that all?"

"Ray, I hardly even looked at it! Just took it off the man and stuffed it in my pocket. I didn't expect you to be interested."

"All right, forget it," I sighed, and turned away.

"Ray! If you're that interested, why don't you try the Centaur Embassy? They'd probably know where one of their officers is staying in town—you know how strict they are."

"I do," I agreed grimly. "Thanks for the suggestion. I may just do that."

And, when another hour's cogitation had failed to turn up a better proposal, I decided I should.

I was thoroughly depressed as I sat hunched up in the back of the cab I'd called to take me to the Centaur Embassy. For years past, I'd assumed that my mind was as good and smoothly functioning as most people's, and a sight better than most. I'd enjoyed the extra advantage of Thoder's teaching, and even if I hadn't been the best of his disciples—

I corrected that: pupils—I'd taken it for granted that I'd absorbed enough of what he showed me to have an edge over less fortunate folk.

Here, now, was a situation tailor-made to test my skills in that area—and I was floundering as helplessly as any Centaur lost in a strange town. I resolved that I wasn't going to behave Centaur-fashion if I found the key to this mental maze. I wasn't immediately going to pretend that I'd never been at a loss at all, the way Centaurs did if they had to demean themselves and ask guidance from foreigners. No, I was going to make a private promise and stick to it: I'd seek out Thoder and do something to recover the psychological techniques I'd neglected so long I was in danger of losing them.

Wait.

There was another of the puzzling visions surfacing in my memory. Four Centaurs, lost, unable to find their way. It was a predictable concomitant of the metaphor I'd employed to reinforce my decision with self-contempt, but it had a strange vividness. Something else out of this dream, to which I was so readily ascribing other improbabilities?

Or a real memory breaking through from limbo?

Uncertain, I peered ahead to see how far I still was from the Centaur Embassy. Just coming into sight around the curve of the canal. Why weren't its lighted signs on?

Why should they be, in the middle of the day?

Why should I expect them to be?

Exactly in the manner in which the wind begins to lift away drifted dust concealing something on the Martian desert, these tantalising clues were now hinting at an underlying pattern. For some as yet indefinable reason I knew it was wrong, perhaps dangerous, for me to go to the Embassy. I stopped the cab with a shaking hand, paid it off and made for the nearest sidewalk lock.

Instead of entering it, however, I paused and glanced at the Embassy one more time. I *had* last seen it with its big gaudy signs illuminated. And, what was more, from approximately this angle and this distance. Where had I come from, to get here?

That eluded me for the present. I made to open the lock and checked afresh. I hadn't gone in to the sidewalk; I'd stayed on the street. This confirmed that it was night-time. Traffic was sparse anywhere on Mars compared with most human worlds, but by day it was thick enough to make walking in the roadways of a town a dangerous pastime.

From here to—well, quite likely the Old Temple. This kept recurring and recurring in my thoughts with enough insistence to make it the best possibility by lightyears.

The Old Temple lacked any sort of door or window. The discoverers had come down to floor-level from above, using ladders; then, of course, sand-drifts had banked clear to its top. When they were building Zond, they drove a tunnel under the street, rising into the middle of the mysterious building. I recalled the tunnel as being large, bright, decorated with handsome murals by a native Martian painter —gay mineral glazes baked into tile.

I found sifted sand an inch deep underfoot, half the fluorescents extinguished, many of the tiles from the murals missing without even an attempt being made to replace them; there were just blank patches showing the grey of the cement used to affix them. A sort of panic gripped me. What was becoming of my home world while I gallivanted around the stars?

Climbing the steps at the far end of the tunnel, I found an apathetic guide reciting an account of the Temple's discovery to a group of young Earthsiders about seven or eight years old—mid-teens, Earth-style. To judge from the comments of those nearest me, they were more concerned with the fact that they were being shown around by a human instead of being given pre-programmed autoguides to play over through earphones, as in an Earthside museum, and they weren't greatly impressed.

There were no other Martians here, of course. Even the guide wasn't a Martian, but an elderly Earthborn woman. Did any Martians ever visit this planetary shrine nowadays? The only other visitors were a scholarly pair of Bears with the indefinable stamp of teachers on sabbatical leave.

To distract myself from the droning voice of the guide, I strode to the far end of the floor and occupied myself in a study of the fifteen artefacts ranged in argon-filled pressurised cases to protect them from further decay. They were time-gnawed beyond recognition, even assuming they had ever served a function comprehensible to human beings. Once, I seemed to recall, I'd stared at them in awe, drawn on the flat photos of them sold at the automat alongside— I couldn't afford the more expensive solido pictures also available when I was a kid—my own reconstructions of their original form . . .

Now they were just lumps: aluminum, steel, complex plastics, glasses opaqued from millennia of radiation. I looked at the explanatory texts—*First discovered, 34 mm. x 107 mm., bluish-grey, irregular; mostly steel, five rods of glass through left end, diameters 2 mm., 4.1 mm., 1.6 mm., 1.9 mm., 2.8 mm.; weight of whole artefact* . . .

Yes, that was the only thing we knew about them after all these years: they were too regular to be natural formations.

"Excuse me!" The elderly guide was bellowing up at me from somewhere around my left elbow, trying to make me move over so she could spiel about the display and get rid of her miserable band of children. I went. All the way out, back to the tunnel. I felt sick.

Wandering aimlessly along the damaged mural, I reached out and touched the tiles around the gaps in the picture, to see if any more were loose, wondering why those that fell had been taken—or thrown—away instead being stuck back in place. With my fingertips I pried at each gap's edge in turn.

Something ought to be done about this, as about the leaking roof I'd seen . . . or dreamed I'd seen . . .

That one gave to the touch! I came back from my musing with a start, expecting to hear a thud as a dislodged tile landed in the sand underfoot. No tile fell. Yet I was certain I'd felt a movement—was it this tile, the last I'd touched, or the one before?

The one before. But the sense in which it moved wasn't that of coming away. It stayed stuck fast in place; the entire section of wall to which it was attached swung very slowly outward towards me.

Beyond, a small concealed room to which this formed the door: bare, lit by a single high fluorescent and containing among a few other chairs of ordinary plastic one special chair, its back high as my own shoulder, chipped rather than carved from a block of Martian stone.

Memory came surging back on the instant, violent as the blasting of rockets, and I stood in a dream of bewilderment as I struggled to organise the facts available to me. I had no way of telling how long I might have stayed rooted to the spot, for I was interrupted.

The room also held a man. A Centaur, wearing major's insignia. At my intrusion he had gasped and swung to face me; during my spasm of total dissociation he had snatched at a weapon lying on the seat of the stone chair. A nerve-whip.

"Come in, Engineer Mallin!" he rasped. "Pull the door to behind you!" And, when I failed to stir, he added, "Move, you fool! You of all people should know I can use this thing!"

And when I still did not move, he used it.

X

THE DOOR WAS AJAR. At any moment someone might enter the tunnel—perhaps one of the bored children being shown over the Old Temple, eager to get away at the earliest possible opportunity—see it, come to investigate. Some such consideration must have made the major put his whip on medium rather than maximum, a setting capable of blotting out a bull's consciousness with pain, let alone a man's. At medium, I should be hurt enough to obey, yet retain sufficient strength to pull the door to, and the time taken would be less than if he rendered me unconscious where I was standing, so that I fell across the threshold and he had to drag me out of the way before he could shut the door himself.

Thus far I could read the major's thoughts as clearly as a page of print. Beyond that point I could only make guesses based on his open-mouthed expression of amazement and disbelief. When he whipped me, I might have been expected to double over like a man punched hard in the solar plexus. Instead, he was the one who got hit—full on the front of the throat, the choking blow with the stiff fingers with which a dwarf can disable a giant, just above the Adam's apple. Like most men accustomed to dealing with—well—dwarfs, height six feet or so, he had no mental preparation for the reach of a Martian arm; like all men wary of low gravity, he unconsciously checked his faster movements for fear he should overshoot with them.

But this was only a part of the way I managed to take the whip away from him.

He had seen me freeze into a paralysis of shock as I opened the door, recognised the room and was engulfed by a sandstorm of recovered memory. He had mistakenly thought that all the rest of the time I was standing stockstill I was as petrified as during the first few heartbeats.

Not so. Far more had come blasting into my mind than merely the things that Thoder had tried to hide from me—it had to be Thoder's doing, my loss of yesterday, or at least he must have betrayed me into the hands of the person directly responsible. Barriers due to simple passage of time had been blown to splinters as well as those artificially imposed within the past day. Whole blocks of Thoder's teaching for which I had never found a use before suddenly integrated and offered me escape from this accidental entrapment. Moreover, since I tried them out as childhood exercises I'd acquired the experience of an adult to guide me in their application. I could almost hear him saying what he had drilled into me about pain being a powerful reinforcement.

So, with pain assured . . .

There was the little bead on the string. Glancing at it casually, one would think that between the hole drilled at the top and that drilled at the bottom was a straight line. In fact it was curved thus:). Let the string slacken, the bead slid down to the bottom rapidly. Pull it taut, and the bead stopped.

First I stopped it, to give myself time to analyse and digest the welter of information I'd recovered. I could hear a voice curiously drawling and deep, saying what seemed to be, "Ay . . . ay . . . aynnn . . . jee . . . nn . . . ee . . . aaarrr . . . mmaa . . . all . . . ll . . . ee . . . eennn . . ."

Engineer Mallin. The sound stretched like elastic.

So this was presumably Major Housk, the one who'd been looking for me at home. By implication he'd admitted that he was one of my interrogators of the night before last—indeed, he was the one who used the whip so cruelly. I ought to turn the tables. The way offered itself.

Pain was a reinforcement. I gathered my energies to take advantage of the certainty of violent pain, instructing myself in this elongated moment of now what I should do. When I was sure I would not miss with my outstretched fingers, but find the vulnerable area of his throat precisely, I prepared to let the string slacken to the fullest extent compatible with consciousness, so that the instant the first pain-messages were reported to my mind I would switch modes and my *now* would leap ahead at dozens of times the normal rate, dulling the pain at the subliminal level until I was safely in possession of the whip.

Of course, I had to return to a normal mode of perception before he could recover; otherwise he would have found me sluggish and easy prey. The return brought the aftermath of the whipping into temporal focus. I gasped and choked and my vision swam, but I was able to see that Housk was in worse condition and I could spare the time to get to and shut the door.

I was none too soon. Already the tunnel outside was noisy with the clattering feet and high juvenile voices of the party of children leaving the Temple.

I came back and sat down in the huge stone chair; it was a sort of poetic balancing of the accounts to resume my place as interrogator instead of victim. "Get up," I said to Housk, prodding him with my toe.

He moaned thickly. I put the whip on minimum—a level which most people find equivalent to being scalded by boiling water—and gave him a taste of his own medicine. That made him scramble to his feet.

"All the same, you Centaurs," I said bitterly. "Your arrogance must be a mask for insecurity. Still, who wouldn't be insecure, trying to keep his place in the peck-order while running the crazy treadmill you call a society? Is your name Housk?"

He gave a sullen nod. He was a stockily built man, about six-two, with coppery hair, pallid skin and grey eyes.

"Why did you come looking for me this morning?"

Silence. I gave him another short tickling, and when that failed gave him five or six in quick succession. I'd never tried this sort of thing before, But I remembered with diamond clarity how he'd gone about it when interrogating me. I was prepared to be a diligent pupil in his methods.

Cringing, he forced out words. "We—we had to get hold of you again!"

"You'd had me already, for several hours. Clearer!"

Sweat ran down his face in revolting streams. "We didn't think anyone could have held out for so long—we thought you must have been telling the truth!"

"What made you change your mind?" I hefted the whip, but now he was talking I didn't need to use it.

"Orders came . . ." He gulped and clutched his belly.

"What orders? Who from?"

"From—home . . ." He closed his eyes and swayed; evidently these trickling admissions were, costing him dear. "They said you must know something, and when we found out that you'd been to Nizam—and then you turned out to have been a disciple of Thoder's . . ."

Again that curious term "disciple", when only "pupil" had ever been used by Thoder himself! But I didn't care to pursue a mere academic distinction.

"Been watching me pretty closely, have you?"

"Uh—some of the time!" More gulping, then a resumption in haste before I could renew the agony. "We didn't find out you were picked up by Nizam until after you'd been reported going to the herald's."

"What was so special about that? Wait, don't tell me. I know that was how you first got on my track—you posed as a distant relative of mine and got the heralds to give you a family tree . . . *Are* we related?"

"Fifth-degree—cousins," he forced out.

"Seems unkind of you to greet your own kinfolk with this whip, then," I grunted. "What made you so eager to get in touch, though? You still haven't explained that."

Mutinously he set his jaw. Obviously this was the limit of his betrayals of the Centaur cause; I'd come to the secret he meant to hang on to.

"Right, we'll take it slowly. For some reason connected

with my having been aboard the *Hippodamia,* you wanted to locate me. The heralds enabled you to identify Ray Mallin, four-space engineer, giving you a key to my background and what family connections I have. You then tortured me to find out whether I knew—well, whatever was so special about the *Hippodamia* on her last trip. Thinking I didn't know, you let me go.

"Whereupon, as a result of further instructions from home, you regret having done so. You discover—how? Perhaps by a hint picked up off those four Centaur spacemen I guided to the heralds—that last night I didn't do the sensible thing and sleep off the effects of my whipping, but went to attend to some business of my own. Tracking back from there, you also discovered that I was retrieved from the sandpile where you left me to drown by this Peter Nizam. Hmm!" I frowned. "You must therefore be keeping a careful watch on him—he assured me no one knew I was at his place." Out of the corner of my eye I looked to see how exact my deductions were, but pain-tension overlay any betraying muscle-twitches in the Centaur's face.

"This leaves one important gap in our explanations. Tell me, what made you want to interrogate me in the first place?"

No reply. I put the whip up to medium and aimed it at his legs. He staggered and his face went pasty-white, but he remained silent.

I copied his sequence of operations, as before, and whipped his genital region. That blasted him open like a crashing spaceship, bringing words in a kind of scream.

"I don't know! Damn you, damn you, I don't *know!* All I was told to do was find you, question you about your last trip, report home—that's all, I swear it, *that's all!*"

Reluctantly I decided that, though disappointing, his claim was likely to be true. Centaurs were trained to uninquisitive obedience; moreover, since at least three parties not counting myself were showing interest in the matter—Housk and his companions, Peter and Lilith and whoever they might represent, and apparently Thoder, though I dared not guess why—the secret underlying the *Hippodamia's* last voyage might well be one the Centaurs wanted to keep from small fry like Housk.

61

Anyhow, this sort of interrogation wasn't on my orbit at all. My nausea from the brief whipping he'd given me on entering this room had faded, but it had been replaced by a worse kind due to the pain I was inflicting. Logic compelled me to put one more question before I desisted, however.

"What were you supposed to find out from me, then? They must have told you that much, at least, or you'd have been looking for a dark star in the Coalsack!"

He shook his head, clamping his jaw tight against the mere idea of further admissions.

I raised the whip.

"Damn you!" The words were a shriek. "Why do you have to make me talk any more? You know all the rest, you must know it, but if they find out I told you any more they'll kill me!"

"Aren't they likely to kill you for talking as freely as you already have?"

He shook his head again and cast his eyes down. "I'll get busted to the ranks, but—but that's a Centaur whip you're holding . . ."

"In other words, who should know better than a Centaur how hard it is to stand out against it?" I scowled at the nasty little weapon. "You have a point there. All right, I've done with you."

He looked at me like a model for one of those little Bear statuettes entitled *Apprehension*, fearing I didn't mean it.

"But beat this fact into your superior's heads, will you? I did not, I do not, and if everyone else I meet is as dumb as you I'm not likely to, know whatever the hell it is you were trying to find out from me! And now—"

I thumbed the whip to maximum and knocked him out. As I knew from recent experience, that was a less cruel action than using the lower settings; it brought merciful release.

Then I searched this extraordinary concealed room, and was scarcely any the wiser. When I interrupted him, Housk had been peering into a gap between two of the rough stones forming the walls, large enough to accept two fingers. All I found in the hole was a triangle of paper torn from the corner of a larger sheet, blank and white. The best idea which occurred to me was that the hole was what they used to call a "mail-drop" in the days of international spies—a place to be checked at intervals for reports from, or orders to, Centaur agents.

Reluctantly concluding that I could learn no more here, I considered my next step. It seemed logical to find out more about Peter Nizam and Lilith Choy. The precept wasn't one which would have satisfied Thoder, but the saying did go, "The enemy of my enemy is my friend," and Nizam wasn't a name Housk had uttered in the tone reserved for one's allies.

As to Thoder . . . When I next saw him, and I fully intended to see him soon, I wasn't going to approach him as a kind of prodigal son, a lamb returning to the teacher's fold. Not by a million lightyears!

XI

I went direct to the mainsurface entrance of Peter and Lilith's penthouse. I considered myself bound to come back to see them anyway—I was still obligated by the charge Peter had laid on me to relay any gossip I might pick up about the *Hippodamia*—but after learning what I had from Housk it seemed to me I had no one else to turn to. Originally my chief intention had been to settle accounts with whoever had kidnapped and nerve-whipped me. That idea had blown away like dust on the wind. If Housk had been acting on orders from "home", that meant this was an affair in which the Centaur government was involved through at least some of its agencies; it would be stupid to put my head down and batter forward on the path I'd first chosen. I needed to know exactly what I'd wandered into.

I hesitated before rapping on the door of the penthouse. I should have thought to make a comweb call first; they might not be in, and I'd have wasted my journey. But I'd been raised under the shadow of the traditional Martian assumption that comwebs were for emergencies—there had never been a full-scale private web established here. Thoder had just acquired a comweb code when I left him to make my first spacetrip. Prior to that, he'd managed without. I'd never had a code of my own, relying on the shared code of the apartment block where I lived. It didn't seem worth the expense when I was so seldom at home.

Well here I was. I might as well stop thinking of un-realised possibilities and rap on the door. In a sense that was another primitive habit, of course. How many things common to virtually all other inhabited worlds were lacking on Mars! Where else had I ever been where people actually knocked on doors instead of announcing themselves to a door-scanner?

I was beginning to carp continually at the way Mars seemed to have been bypassed: shortage of comwebs, lack of door-scanners, neglect of sidewalk glass, no maintenance in the district of Zond which I hailed from, no Martians go-ing to admire the unique relics in the Old Temple . . .

The door was opened. That is to say, the outer, opaque panel of the pressure lock was freed so that I could slide it back, squeaking a little from the sand in its grooves, and I could see Lilith beyond the inner, transparent panel. Her face showed tense excitement. But only for seconds. As soon as she recognised me, she let dismay show through.

Faintly from within the apartment I heard Peter calling: "He's in good time—early, in fact!"

"It isn't him," Lilith replied. "It's—uh—Ray Mallin."

I missed Peter's next remark owing to the dense wet air flooding into the lock; it muffled my hearing as efficiently as cottonwool before I adjusted to it, clearing my Eustachians with loud swallows. The pressure meter sped around its dial to the figure 3, and I expected the inner door to slide back. It didn't. The needle went to 2, to 1, and finally all the way to sea-level, zero, before I was able to pass into the interior.

Atmosphere like this was clammy and thick as fog to me. I was bewildered. I was sure that on my previous visit the pressure had only been 3, or thereabouts. Peter and Lilith were young and healthy—why should they go to the need-less expense of having sea-level air in here at all? The price went up with the square of the meter-reading below the Martian standard of 10. Every breath they took cost them a hundred times what it cost me in my apartment.

But I had no chance to worry further about this anomaly. Peter had emerged into plain sight from a room over on my left, closing its door behind him a little too quickly, as if he were agitated. Also his greeting to me rang falsely hearty.

"Good to see you again! Are you completely recovered?"

"Yes, thank you," I said grimly. I waited.

"Ah—what brings you back?" he said at random when the pause had become unbearable.

"Have you forgotten? You laid a charge on me. I committed myself to an obligation, and you held me to it."

"Oh! That's very kind of you," Lilith said. She also was nervous about something; her tiny hands were pressed together apparently against the risk of them trembling visibly. "But it's no longer necessary."

"That's so!" Peter confirmed. "We—uh—we got what we wanted from another source. So please consider yourself freed from the charge, with our grateful thanks!"

His eyes strayed to the door, for all the galaxy as if he hoped to be able to see clear through it.

It didn't take much imagination to work out that they were in the same plight as Thoder had been in. They were expecting someone whose presence they preferred not to advertise. Within the bounds of hospitality and politeness they wanted very much to get me out of the way before the important visitor showed up. But they dared not simply tell me to go to hell, because that in itself was a giveaway.

Thoder's visitor had been Lugath, the last person I'd ever have guessed at. I wondered if Peter and Lilith's guest would be someone equally improbable—Housk, for example. I resolved to be extremely obtuse and spin out my stay until they actually threw me off the premises.

"A lot of things have been happening since I left here yesterday," I began at random. "Remember you correctly deduced that when you found me by the Old Temple I'd been worked over with a nerve-whip? Well, I caught up with the people who did it to me."

That sparked interest in both of them, creating a short-lived dilemma. They'd admitted that they were looking for the Martian engineer who'd shipped home from Durrith with Lugath; it followed logically that they'd be interested in others on the same errand. But the spark was a brief one, and didn't lead to the response I'd hoped for. Presumably, then, they had information about the subject already.

Possibly they'd had it when I was here yesterday. They had, after all, displayed remarkably little concern about the way in which I'd arrived on the sandpile, half-drowned.

The dilemma of choice between hearing what I had to say and getting rid of me resolved in favour of the latter. But they were still thinking of an excuse when there came a sound that illuminated whole new areas for me, accounting in particular for the sea-level pressure in the apartment.

From the room over to the left where Peter had been as I arrived, I heard the thin wailing of a very small baby.

They exchanged horrified glances. Then Peter thrust his fingers through his close-curled hair and shrugged.

"I'm sorry we're not being very welcoming," he said. "But —uh—we're minding a child for some friends of ours, and the poor thing seems to be a bit sickly. We're waiting for a doctor right now. Supposed to have been here two or three minutes ago, actually."

"I do hope you understand," Lilith chimed in, jumping enthusiastically into the spirit of the deception. I was sure beyond doubt it was a lie they were telling. But why bother to take such elaborate precautions over the presence of a baby?

"It's a big responsibility looking after someone else's kid," Peter amplified. "We've been dreadfully worried, and—"

Knock, knock, knock. They both started; decided there was no help for it; muttered an apology and went together to open the door.

"Good of you to come, *doctor!*" Peter exclaimed cheerfully. The stress on the last word was too heavy. The newcomer was no doctor, definitely. They were just hoping he would catch on to the cover-story and play along.

"The poor thing's not at all well, and we felt a doctor must see him right away!" That was Lilith, rubbing in the message. It got across.

"Don't worry about him," the visitor called through the transparent inner panel of the lock as the air thickened around him. "I'm sure it's nothing serious!"

He was a bulky man in plain brown outdoor clothing, peeling off his mask to reveal a square face, mid-brown complexion, slight red wind-chapping across his forehead.

Wind-chapping! In that case he wasn't a resident of this planet, or at any rate he hadn't been here very long. The cold dry Martian wind always affected new arrivals like this, but a matter of a few months almost invariably saw the skin harden and adjust. I re-heard by an exercise of memory the few words he'd uttered. From his accent, he wasn't any kind of a local man. He wasn't even an Earthman, as one might have expected.

I addressed him in the most fiercely accented Bear dialect I could manage.

"Gude af'noon, dooktoor!"

He disciplined himself well, for a Bear, but he didn't dare go as far as challenging me on the point and denying his nationality. He merely grunted and demanded of Lilith where the child was, taking extra pains to mask his dialect inflections and not quite managing it.

I didn't press matters any further. I stood aside as she led him into the room with the baby. By now the crying had taken on a distinctly fractious note, and I would have laid bets on the kid not being more than fifteen days old.

That young? Sick enough to need a doctor, yet abandoned by the parents into the care of friends? Even if I hadn't already had grounds to be suspicious of Peter and Lilith's good faith, I'd have had trouble swallowing such a tale.

Like most proverbs, the saying about the enemy of my enemy had holes in it. I relinquished my half-formed intention of being as open with these two as they had been with me yesterday, and offering to trade what assistance I could render for explanations of their interest in the *Hippodamia*. It was a blow—I'd been prepared to take them at face value and indeed to like them, since they'd treated me better than even Thoder, who was the last person I'd have expected to play on me the kind of dirty trick I'd suffered last night.

I'd have to be satisfied with another element of the puzzle, although it aggravated my difficulties. They had something to hide, and it led to Bear involvement in the mystery.

Centaurs, Earthsiders, Martians—apparently, considering

that Lugath had come to see Thoder—and now Bears? The possible ramifications were beginning to scare me. Not being a man accustomed to anger, I was going to find it difficult to continue without being tempted to opt out and hope nothing further would happen to me.

Peter was standing before me in acute anxiety. Had he something more to say?

He had, and in another few seconds plucked up the courage to utter it.

"Look—ah—it was very kind of you to come back and offer this information to us, even though it turned out not to be necessary any longer. I'm most impressed with the standard of Martian honour, and I want to apologise for Lilith's and my seeming to doubt you yesterday."

But this was all smokescreen; he had a point still waiting to be made.

"Since in a sense you haven't discharged the obligation, though," he went on, "perhaps you'd allow me to ask you to —ah—refrain from mentioning the fact that . . ."

Abruptly I was furious. I strode towards him, towering above his gravity-stunted form. "Are you treating Martian obligations as a kind of—of *money*? This one worth so much, that one worth so much less, give me my correct change?"

"No, I didn't mean—"

"Then what in the cosmos *did* you mean?" I could see now a purpose to which to turn my fury, even though it had come on me involuntarily. Let him think he'd insulted me and driven me away, rather than that I'd been clever enough to see through his flimsy deceptions. Perhaps he might not even expect me to draw conclusions from the presence of a Bear with secrets to keep. "It's the kind of sordid commercial nonsense we Martians have come to expect from Earthsiders! If you're going to spend long on my planet, you'll have to cure yourself of these shabby second-rate ideas!"

There was a moment of silence. "I'm sorry," he said at last, in such a miserable tone I almost relented. "Please put it down to my ignorance of your traditions."

"I'm not ignorant of yours," I said. "I know more about them than I care to. Goodbye!"

Outside in the blessedly thin natural air, feeling the clammy
chill of excessive moisture inside my clothing, I reviewed
my predicament. My plan to appeal to Peter and Lilith
had come to nothing. I'd learned nothing of any great help
from Housk. I must go and beard Thoder again, there was
no alternative. And this time I was going to be totally on
guard against him. Whatever he'd become, he was no longer
the gentle, much-respected teacher of my childhood.

XII

AND YET I hesitated. For all that Thoder was integrated
into the net weaving around me, so that I'd become suspicious of him too—even afraid—unless he had *been* changed,
forcibly, I couldn't imagine his nature altering completely. I'd
sensed nothing worse, talking to him yesterday, than this
elusiveness due to his not wanting me to see Lugath when
he arrived. Otherwise he'd been the same as ever.

On the other hand I couldn't conceive any alternative to
the assumption that he'd tampered with my memory, or arranged for it to be done, when I flaked out from the effects
of the nerve-whipping combined with the shock of recognising Lugath.

Granted that: could I ascribe him any honorable motive
for the action?

He'd said I was in possession of much more data than
I consciously knew. Suppose he was aware of the significance
of events, and feared that I might inadvertently let slip some
clue which would alert another interested party—say, the
Bear faction concerned—leading to another such night as
I'd spent at the mercy of Housk and his companions, being
interrogated under torture?

It was an incredibly slim chain of reasoning. And yet
there was something un-Thoder-like about the speed with
which the mental barriers had dissolved. Possibly the gap
in my memory had been designed to last only a short time.
There were several indications to this effect. For one thing,
the gap had been left open, not masked by false memories;
even if I hadn't recovered some random fragments of the
missing experience and mistaken them for elements in a vivid

dream, I'd soon enough have begun to worry when I noticed the date.

And for another, when the memory did come back, an immense number of other things came with it. Simply to say that when I found myself confronting Housk I was shocked into right action was inadequate. I'd performed—accurately and immediately—mental gymnastics such as I hadn't tried for years, and had never fully mastered even under Thoder's patient tuition as a boy.

As though Thoder had wanted to compensate me in some fashion for his intrusion on my inmost privacy.

In that case: was his purpose as straightforward as a desire to keep me from interfering while in pursuit of revenge? I'd made it clear that I wouldn't rest easy until I'd squared accounts with the screened interrogators. Knowing far more than I, he might have acted from a double motive: partly to protect me, partly to stop me meddling.

He ought to have been open instead of going this round-about road, I thought resentfully, and at once saw I was being foolish. It was no good saying he "ought" to have been frank. I'd collapsed on his floor and it must have been several hours before my consciousness was again accessible; he must have had business with Lugath which would anyhow have prevented him from indulging in long complicated explanations for my benefit; and besides, we'd not met for many years—why should he automatically assume that as an ex-pupil I was to be trusted with important secrets?

Yet his connection with Lugath had a sinister aura. Why should an Earthman pose as a Centaur—and do it well enough to pass among Centaurs, giving himself away only to me by a sheer fluke? All the conceivable explanations were way off the orbit you'd expect an unassuming Martian teacher to fly.

I came back, and back, and back to the conclusion that Thoder was no longer—possibly had not been when I studied under him—a mere teacher.

The necessity of challenging him was inescapable. Once more, though, I felt myself retreating in order to find a new line of advance. The years during which I hadn't seen, had barely even thought of, Thodor were taking on an almost solid reality for me. I ought to find out when and under what circumstances he had left the house in the run-down quarter where I'd been raised, gone to this well-maintained home in a district frequented by offworlders. I must construct a kind of mental bridge across the intervening years.

So: before meeting him again, I had to return to that little tributary of the town where the sand piled high on the roof and strained the pylons into alarming bows.

I might as well, in fact, call again on Yuma: butter him up with compliments on his memory and thanks for putting me in touch with my fifth-degree cousin Major Housk, in the hope that his eidetic recall would short-circuit an otherwise tedious process of locating and questioning people who had known Thoder in the old days.

Gules, a helium atom or, differenced by a label argent charged with three lozenges of the first. I had no idea whose bearing that was, but it took only an elementary knowledge of heraldry to tell me whose it was likely to be. The stylised atom—two ellipses intersecting at right angles around a nucleus—suggested a physicist; the label indicated an eldest son; the three lozenges superimposed on the difference most probably referred to a connection by marriage with some illustrious bearer of them as a chief device.

Hmmm . . . In a cockeyed fashion this ancient symbolic language could be extremely informative. No wonder the Centaurs, with their emphasis on kinship and their vast network of patronage, had taken it up in such a big way. And, come to that, no wonder the Bears tended to look on it as silly. They were so completely the reverse of the Centaurs. Why, I was sure that half the children of my Bear friends weren't the offspring of their mother's husband, and nobody gave a damn. A child was a child was a child, to Bears. Paternity was more or less irrelevant.

That was further than I, as a Martian, could go in admiring Bear rather than Centaur customs. Even so, forced to make a choice, I couldn't deny which I would prefer.

The display changed. Barré of vert and argent, on an inescutcheon engrailed sable, a griffin of the first crowned and collared of the second. I stared at it, baffled, for some time before concluding that while it could occasionally be illuminating heraldic symbology could also be damnaby obscure.

The door was closed, but not of course locked. It wasn't a Martian habit to lock doors. On impulse I checked the fist I was about to bang against it, and instead slid it quietly back and stepped inside.

It was little darker here than out on the sidewalk; sand-clearance was overdue everywhere in the district, and a good half of the transparent roof-panels were covered. I didn't have to wait for my eyes to adjust, but could see clearly at once.

I could also hear voices: Yuma's and that of Zond King of Arms. Very quietly I crept to the door of the room in which they were talking.

"We'll simply *have* to organise a fresh grant of arms for this character!" the woman was saying. "Thirty-two quarterings, five of them quartered and one of the quartered quarters quartered again—Gehenna, it's worse than the Portuguese royal family!"

"We can't," Yuma responded in a tone like a vocalised shrug. "He hasn't done anything to deserve a grant of arms."

"It's all very well for you, with your eidetic memory," came the acid reply. "I have not only to blazon the damned thing but actually put it on paper. What's the use of arms you have to read with a microscope?"

"Well, in a sense it is a kind of microscope, isn't it?" Yuma murmured, and the woman gave a harsh chuckle. The joke escaped me completely. Then she sighed.

"You're quite right, of course. Still, with all this talent in his ancestry you'd think he'd do something with his life instead of vegetating."

"He's busy raising a family," Yuma said, and continued with sly malice, "How are you going to enjoy blazoning his kids' arms, incidentally? His wife is a Boigny de Chavannes with two quartered quarterings of her own."

"Oh, shut up." A rustling of papers, and: "Gehenna! Go find me a couple of square inches of potent-counter-potent, will you? The smallest size we have in stock."

I took one long noiseless stride back to the middle of

the vestibule, reached behind me with one hand as if I'd this second entered and pushed the door to and occupied the brief interval before Yuma appeared in recalling that potent-counter-potent was an obscure device like rows of interlocked capital T's set head-to-head.

Yuma saw me, blinked, identified me, and gave an uncertain smile. "Ah—can I help you?" he inquired.

"Who is it?" called the woman.

"Ray Mallin, who was here yesterday!"

"Uh-huh. Don't be too long with that stuff, will you? I need it for the second arms in the dexter quarter."

Yuma sighed. Before he could speak again, I did. I said, "As a matter of fact I didn't come about anything important, so don't let me hold you up."

"Thanks." He crossed the vestibule to a wall-hung cupboard which I recalled from my days as Thoder's pupil; then, it had held some of the many objects he used to dramatise his precepts for young children, whereas now it was stuffed to overflowing with tiny jars of paint, rolls of gold and silver leaf, and pockets of heraldic devices and field-patterns in various sizes from large to nearly invisible.

While he sorted through several packets in search of the one he wanted, I continued, "I really came to thank you and let you know I did get in touch with my cousin from Centaurus."

"Major Housk?" Yuma said. "Running short of those," he added to himself, singling out a packet of inch-high fleurs de lys in assorted heraldic colours and putting it back on the shelf.

"You must have an amazing memory," I told him warmly.

"I'm an eidetic," he shrugged. "Some people are, some aren't. It's nothing I can take credit for." He found what he wanted, a bit of plioform with the design on it, which could be trimmed to size and pasted in the appropriate space on an escutcheon.

Not easily reached by flattery, that was clear. I cast around for a way of continuing the subject, and at once saw an obvious path. "But your ancestors must have been remarkable people to endow you with the talent! You must have a fascinating genealogy."

I could tell I'd broken through by the casual—too casual

—tone of his reply. "I guess it is pretty interesting. Though since it's my own I'm prejudiced about it."

"Does your family go back a long way on Mars?"

Three-quarters of an hour, it took for him to explain all the ramifications of his family. It wasn't boredom which made me struggle to conceal impatience—he was an expert in love with his job, and it's always a pleasure to hear enthusiasts holding forth. Besides, his family *was* interesting; it hailed from six different continents on Earth and all the sizeable towns on Mars.

I was, however, itching to work around to the subject of Thoder, and finally had to cut the corners off his orbit. I asked, straight out, how come Zond King of Arms had taken over Thoder's old home.

"Thoder?" Yuma blinked at me. "Now there's a man with an ancestry! I worked his geneology through out of curiosity and it doesn't show anything like the strains you'd expect to produce a—"

I steered him gently back to my question.

"Why, the house just came available at the right time. Thoder was offered a job at the College of Serendipity—"

"*What?*"

"Oh, you're thinking of what my boss told you: that he'd retired. In the literal sense he has—he's Professor Emeritus, doesn't do much actual teaching any more but gives a lecture course . . ."

"At the College of Serendipity?"

"Yes." Yuma was puzzled at the intensity of my reaction. "That's an institute up on main surface, about five miles—"

"I know where it is, thank you," I said grimly.

I also knew what it was. Insofar as there was anything to appeal to Bears, it was the College of Serendipity, a crank organisation of the purest water. Like all gamblers, Bears tended to objectify the concept of "luck", to be superstitious, to carry charms, to perform meaningless little rituals. The most high-sounding term for luck was *serendipity*, the faculty of chancing upon good fortune; the College, believe it or not, claimed to teach you how to be lucky!

No, Thoder *couldn't* have sunk to that level—I wouldn't let myself credit it for a single moment!

XIII

BEFORE I COULD question him further, though, Yuma was called back to work by his boss. I spent a little while longer wandering around the neighbourhood looking for anybody else who might remember Thoder and tell me more about his departure, but I found only casual acquaintances who didn't miss him particularly.

At last I rebuked myself for wasting time. I was using the excuse of making inquiries about him in order to postpone a direct confrontation. Exactly as I had done yesterday, I hailed a cab and set off to his new address.

It was an eerie sensation to be going past all the same places in the same sequence as previously, as though I were trapped in a sort of temporal echo, or following a spiral around a centre, each traverse of the repeating pathway bringing me fractionally closer to enlightenment: Old Temple to Grand Canal Apartments to the heralds' place to Thoder's . . .

The same again tomorrow, the day after, and indefinitely?

The sense of being caught in an echo was redoubled when I once more stood face to face with Thoder. He had precisely the air of disappointment Lilith had betrayed, due to my not being the person expected at this time; likewise, he was as astonished as she had been at my being who I was. He was agitated for certain, or he'd have kept a tighter rein on his emotions.

But instead of acting as Lilith and Peter had done, and attempting to cover up with a hollow falsehood, he sighed and resigned himself to the course of events. Standing back from the door, he silently gestured for me to enter. I complied warily, wondering if I was about to be ambushed.

"So it didn't work," he said when he had pulled the door to.

"No, it didn't work." I omitted to explain what had caused it to break down. "So I'm back, and this time I'd like a civiller welcome than I had from you yesterday."

Another sign as he waved for me to enter the room where

we had talked before. "Yes . . . It's very seldom that I panic, but then it's also very seldom that I become involved in events which can affect the whole of human history. Are you used to that? I imagine not, from what you told me last evening."

He settled in his chair with his careful old-man precision. "I don't know whether you now harbour a grudge against me," he went on, "or whether you've been able to think the matter through with proper clarity and assess my motives. Hm?"

I weighed my words. "If you'd intended me to forget permanently, you're skilled enough to have done a thorough job instead of a patchwork one liable to be smashed accidentally. On the other hand, it's out of character for you to have done it at all." I hesitated. "Though that isn't a very persuasive argument, because I've learned something about you which makes me think you're *living* out of character nowadays."

"Am I?" He chuckled. "How's that?"

"Are you really lecturing at the College of Serendipity?"

"Yes, why not? I'm Professor Emeritus of life-adjustment there." The assertion was almost belligerent, and I discerned a shadow passing across his face—but it might have been illusory.

"Why not?" I echoed. "Well . . . never mind. The important thing is this: last night you tampered very extensively with my memory, blotting out the better part of thirty-six hours' recall. What in the name of the Zodiac did you do it for?"

"It seemed the kindest thing to let you carry on with your normal life between trips, rather than risk being crushed between the millstones of gigantic opposed forces like a grain of corn."

"I guess you thought it was too easy to be frank with me!"

"I considered it." He didn't blink. "Lugath argued against the idea—he thinks you showed up too conveniently on Durrith—but that wasn't what decided me. I couldn't have raised your consciousness even to light trance level before you'd slept away three or four hours. You'd been nerve-whipped worse than anyone else I'd ever seen. Moreover, as you yourself pointed out—quoting me!—pain is a reinforcement. You'd had enough pain to disconnect your top-level drives and key you into a positive dynamo of vengeance-need."

"You coin a good phrase," I taunted. "So it was all done for my own sweet sake and I have no business coming back to complain to you—is that it?" I leaned forward.

"For pity's sake, why don't you stop prevaricating and admit that you were afraid I'd meddle in something too big for me and foul it up?"

He didn't reply at once. He hoisted himself to his feet and crossed to the window, looking both ways along the sidewalk. Returning, he stood gazing down at me while I met his eyes fixedly.

"All right," he said abruptly. "I'd not have said you were one of my most successful pupils, but you're a long way from stupid, and the fact that you came back in a fit state to talk instead of jumping to the conclusion that I was a villain and a traitor indicates a passable degree of rationality. What's more, the way things are turning out we shall need every ounce of help we can get . . ." He combed his white hair with his thin gnarled fingers.

"What do you make of the affair you've stumbled into, so far?"

"Damnably little. Something about the *Hippodamia*'s last trip is worrying the Centaurs—the fact that Lugath is apparently an Earthman posing as a Centaur connects but doesn't explain. Earthsiders are interested in whatever it is, and I think Bears also, and Martians in the shape of yourself. Presumably it's enormous. You just said it could affect the whole of history. How?"

He sat down again, shaking his head. "So much to make clear!" he grumbled. "I'm getting old, Ray, and I find it difficult to know where to begin."

"The beginning might be a good place!"

"That way it could take weeks . . . Tackle it from this point, perhaps. Ray, how does it feel to be a young Martian in this day and age?"

"Pretty depressing," I said. I instanced reasons: the shabbiness, the neglect, the second-best-will-do attitude I saw all around me; the absence of such a thing as Martian nationality even though we couldn't live in comfort on Earth, our legal home world; even the way someone like Peter could cheapen the honorable traditions we'd developed when we were struggling pioneers breaking the back of a hostile planet.

"There's more to it than you can see. You're too close and too involved." Thoder leaned back and put his fingertips together, a pose I remembered from innumerable childhood lectures. "But to show you clearly why there's more, and what that extra involves, I shall have to set the scene. Name me a major scientific breakthrough of the past century."

I hesitated, and he forestalled my answer. "I'm sorry. I still have this lifetime habit of making other people do the work, so that it fixes clearly in their minds. I'll save you the trouble. There has been *no* major scientific breakthrough since the beginning of the twenty-second century, when we established the four-space drive on a reliable footing and turned interstellar travel from an adventure into a matter of routine."

"But surely—"

"I'm not arguing, Ray. I'm telling you. It is even a tenable thesis that the last new concept in human thinking was Einstein's insight into the equivalence of matter and energy. Step back further yet—*il faut reculer pour mieux sauter*, as I kept telling you when you were a kid."

"One must go back to jump better," I parroted.

"Shut up. Merely because I tend to ramble more as I get older is no excuse for you to do so. There are certain key inventions in human evolution—mental evolution—which one can call totally novel. Name some!"

"Ah . . . The knife, the bow, control of fire, the wheel—"

"Textiles, literacy, the alphabet, numeracy, the invention of money, the liberation of thermal energy, the liberation of nuclear energy, and the computer. There are a few others, but those should indicate to you the points of the curve I'm trying to establish."

I squinted at nothing, visualising a graph with time on the x-axis, log scale, and technological advancement on the y-axis, ditto.

"What you're saying," I ventured after a pause, "is that

we should have had dozens—scores—of comparable new concepts since the Industrial Revolution on Earth."

Thoder almost crowed with delight. "Yes! Yes! Ray, you must have been completing your education since I last saw you—I expected to have to lead you to this by slow and painful stages!"

"Wait a moment!" I objected. "There *have* been dozens. Atomic theory was at least as powerful a tool as the reciprocating engine employing heat-energy—in fact the two were interdependent, because they both relied on developments in chemical—"

"Last century? Last *two* centuries?"

I was silent. Every suggestion that sprang to my mind was open to the charge that it wasn't a new concept but an elaboration of an old one, except the faster-than-light drive. And we'd dealt with that.

"All right, let's tackle another aspect. Do you believe there's a pattern—putting it in wholly subjective terms, a purpose—to human history?"

"You used to tell us that each successive generation formulated such a purpose according to its best knowledge, and had to be prepared for the next generation to alter or even to reject that purpose, and that any other view of human destiny was arbitrary. I've never seen any reason to disagree with what you taught."

"Good," Thoder approved, and added with disturbing emphasis, "I hope for your sake you mean that all the way to the floor of your mind! If you don't—but I'm getting ahead of myself.

"Purpose is essential. Human beings having the mental attitudes they do, once we'd become self-analytical enough to start questioning our motives in human rather than in artificial theological terms we had consciously to create this series of malleable purposes. We hit on one and called it 'progress'."

"An alleged hyperbolic series of events plotted on a graph of which one axis is calibrated in starships and the other in numbers of people undergoing psychotherapy."

"Did *I* say that?" Thoder demanded, and when I nodded he grinned in satisfaction. "A striking phrase—I must revive it! But I'm not out to blast holes in our predecessors' mistakes; it's a futile pastime even though it may be entertaining. Ray, what is our ultimate and absolutely indispensable resource?"

I sat for the space of five of his slow Martian breaths while I thought back and back. I was satisfied now that he had not meant to offend me when he doctored my memory, but would have explained and apologised later, when resolved. Accordingly I wanted to parallel his thinking as closely as I could, so that I would be able to share his conclusions and perhaps give him the help he'd hinted at needing.

"Ourselves," I said finally.

He actually clapped that, hands crisply uttering a sharp explosion. "Our genetic endowment, to make it a little more exact. Now: let me set you one or two more questions, and I think you may very well answer the riddle yourself.

"First: what's the basic handicap of being a Martian?"

"The oxygen-need of the developing embryo," I answered promptly. "If they could lick that, there could really be a Martian race. As it is, we're a kind of amphibian, having to go back to the ocean to breed."

"Hence there are very few of us," he nodded. "Second: what's the fundamental difference between Centaurs and Bears?"

I stared at him. "You know as well as I do! It's not in their physical type, their genetic endowment, or anything—it's solely in the way they organise their society. Bears are permissive and casual, Centaurs rigid and disciplined."

"Precisely. It affects everything, doesn't it—including their family lives, the way they plan and bring up their offspring?" Thoder hunched forward in his chair. "Ray, do you think this is mere happenstance?"

For the space of three more of his breaths, which rang and rang in my ears, I could not find words. Then at last I forced a weak, hopeless complaint past my dry stiff lips.

"What do they think we are, Thoder? Neanderthalers of the twenty-fourth century, due to be cast on the rubbish-dump of evolution and left there—*rotting?*"

XIV

"IF THAT'S how you feel"—Thoder's reproof was sharp—"plainly you didn't mean what you said about human destiny. I'm a Martian too, remember. Our pride and strength has been in transcending hostile circumstances. Here's another—is it to defeat us?"

"Is there any question of victory and defeat? Isn't it a decision that's been taken out of our hands?"

"No, it's not a decision. It's simply an acceptance of the necessity to be what we are. Let me make sure you're talking about the same thing that I am. Martians are . . . ?"

"An experiment that proved abortive." I wiped perspiration off my face. "We were superseded by Bears and Centaurs."

"In effect, yes. But I must condense the rest of it. Look, Ray, we're enormously clever as a species. We can break the most fundamental laws of the universe with impunity and outrace light to the stars. What do we do when we get there? The same things we've been doing for millennia on our planet of origin. As though we'd passed a peak of achievement and begun to decay.

"It was as early as the twenty-first century that the more farsighted planners realised the underlying cause. Gradually Earthside society had begun to homogenise. More and more groups formerly differentiated by linguistic conditioning and local traditions had adopted the universal goal of physical well being and the associated concepts. We had more data than any man could become acquainted with in a lifetime, yet we were unable to deduce novel conclusions from this welter of information. Why? Two hypotheses were proposed, and it so happened that they dovetailed beautifully into a grand overall plan for future human development.

"First it was argued that this social homogeneity led to decline of stimulus. A comfortable tendency to conformity supplanted the urge to explore, break new ground and startle the world with new inventions. The last spectacular surge of technical progress occurred with the four-space drive.

"Also it was argued that the sum of our vaunted ability

to alter our environment, instead of being evolutionarily conditioned by it like non-intelligent creatures, had surpassed our ability to reason about what we were doing. In other words, we needed a new talent, extra psychological muscle, if you like. The talent existed in embryonic form—as witness the not-too-rare ability to grapple with mental concepts such as four-space, which nowhere touches the instinctive world-picture derived from normal sensory data.

"How best to ensure that this double lack was fulfilled?

"Before the advent of the stardrive, people thought we were going to be confined indefinitely to the Old System. Mars was the only other planet here where men might develop their own society and culture, differenced from Earth's by all the factors which have affected you and me. But, as you said, Martians can at best be amphibious, dive back into a high-oxygen environment to bear their children or risk them being morons . . . Yes?"

I'd been thinking in parallel with what he was saying, and scores of hitherto unrelated snippets were combining into a distasteful whole. I said, "If I've followed you correctly, you're about to say that the distinction between Bears and Centaurs is a planned one." Zond King of Arms complaining that with so much talent in his family this man ought to do something more with his life than simply raise children . . . Yuma saying heraldry was a kind of microscope; yes, a means of studying genetic endowment!

"Correct. There was no means of telling whether we yet had sufficient skill to manipulate our heritage and actually breed for the talent we felt was indispensable to further advancement, or whether the workings of chance would throw it up faster." Thoder parodied the tossing of a coin. "So a pair of strongly opposed societies was devised: the Bears, happy-go-lucky, casual, taking life as it came, and the Centaurs, thinking hard about everything and especially about their descendants."

"While the Martians, overtaken by events, were left on one side." I sounded bitter. And why not? I couldn't yet tell how Thoder came by his information, but he spoke with tremendous authority.

"Not entirely. In fact, we exercise influence out of all proportion to our numbers. Our traditions, abortive though the plan behind them was, are still closer to the main line of the future than present-day Earthside customs."

"I guess that's a consolation," I acknowledged sourly. "So —how far are the results to hand now? I take it that we didn't in fact know enough to plan our own breeding, and that the odds are on the Bears to—ah—carry the torch of the future?"

He gazed at me steadily. "No, Ray. Exactly the opposite. We proved to know enough and to spare about our genetic endowment. The talent which the early planners identified has turned up six generations earlier than their most optimistic estimate."

"What? Among *Centaurs?*" I thought of the stiff-necked, narrow-minded authoritarians I knew too well for comfort, and felt a pang of dismay at the idea that the destiny of humanity lay along that road.

Thoder reached behind him to a small locked cabinet; at full stretch of his Martian-long arm, he twisted the combination to open and produced a scroll which he shook out with a flourish and held for me to examine.

It was a coat of arms, divided into quarters. The first and fourth quarters held the two halves of the Tyrant of Centaurus's bearing—the silver stars and comets on black, the tiger's head. The other two quarters displayed devices whose significance I didn't recognize.

"Are you trying to tell me," I said with astonishment, "that the Tyrant of Centaurus has the talent?"

"In little. You know your recent history, I'm sure—you know that in their singleminded determination to make Centaur society an absolutely planned one people overreached themselves and made ghastly false estimates, bringing economic crisis and near-disaster, until the pressure of circumstances threw up the first Tyrant, Boris ben Solomon. He confounded the predictions rife about Centaur collapse —people were pointing to the Bears' capacity for muddling through and saying this was obviously the course to pursue, and Tyrant Boris made them eat their words . . . But of course this isn't the bearing of the present Tyrant Basil."

"Whose, then? Not one of his sons—they'd bear their father's arms with a difference until he died or abdicated."

"Strictly that's so. I didn't know you'd studied heraldry,

but— Never mind that!" Thoder rolled up the arms. "Bluntly: if it were ever granted, which is something I hope devoutly won't happen, this bearing would belong to the son of a rather remarkable courtesan who at the age of seventeen has—ah—*contrived* a morganatic marriage with the Tyrant Presumptive, Basil's eldest son Barnaby."

"You said," I mused aloud, "that you hope the arms won't ever be granted. Because you don't want Tyrant Basil to recognise his grandson as legitimate, or—?" I stopped dead.

"Yes?" Thoder prompted gently.

"Are you trying to tell me that this child was aboard the *Hippodamia?*" *Tamer of horses, hence: tamer of Centaurs!* "That he's been kidnapped from his parents and brought to Mars?"

"It's not as cruel as you think," Thoder parried. "There were twins, a boy and a girl, but the mother and father don't know—the delivery was Caesarean and under anaesthetic. And the girl is carrying enough of the endowment to make her an exceptional child, though only the boy has the whole of it."

"But you can't keep that sort of thing secret! They must know! Why else would orders have come from Centaurus to track me down and question me under torture about the *Hippodamia?*"

A long pause followed. Finally Thoder said, "We're sure they don't know the full story, but . . . Well, Lugath's engineer, whom you replaced, fell sick with Larchman's disease. As you probably know, it brings fever and vociferous delirium. Lugath dared not risk trying to take him off Durrith. He banked on the fact that the sick man was himself not party to the whole secret, engaged you, and ran for it. But in hospital on Durrith the engineer must have let slip enough hints in his ravings to alert the Centaur authorities.

"Also, of course, Bears and Centaurs *and* Earthsiders have secret agents in each other's territories."

"Like Lugath?"

"His status is irrelevant, and so is mine!" Thoder said sharply, then relented. "Oh—yes, I suppose you'd class us as such. But not in the sense of 'spy'. We're . . . instruments of the planners responsible for mapping out mankind's future. The point I was driving at was that knowledge of genetics isn't a Centaur monopoly. Bears have wondered for a long time about the talents emerging in Boris's descendants, and— There he is!"

He jumped from his chair with incongruous sprightliness for a staid old man and hurried to reach the door before his visitor could knock. It was, of course, Lugath.

He stared at me in dismay, and Thoder launched into a long justification of his action in admitting me to the secret he claimed was so well-kept. Lugath contained himself for some minutes, but finally cut the old man short.

"The hell with this!" he rasped. "The kid has gone, and that's beyond doubt. So either the Centaurs have taken him back, or—or someone else has interfered. How in the galaxy do we trace him without alerting Bears, Centaurs and everybody from here to Sagittarius?"

Thoder glanced at me. "You don't approve of what we're doing, do you, Ray? Perhaps you're glad to hear we've lost track of the baby? I grant that in some sense it's inhuman to do as we've done. But consider: when he grows up he'll have an IQ at the limits of the measurable, empathy topping 2000, Weigand scale, and virtually every heritable talent from music to mathematics, *all transmissible to his descendants!* You want that to be a monopoly for the rigid, pompous, narrowminded Centaurs?"

I hesitated. He'd practically read my mind. My first reaction had been to recall all the rumours I'd heard about kidnapping for slavery, and to wonder how many of them were founded on actual events like this. I was repelled— yet this was gentle, wise old Thoder, whom I'd known since boyhood.

"What's your plan, then?" I whispered.

"To educate him on Mars. Then, when he's grown, to use the random mixing of genetic lines available in Bear society to spread a kind of ferment through half the human race."

Was that an admirable plan for mankind's evolution, or a piece of callous bloodstock breeding more suited to raising domestic animals? I was still at a loss. Perhaps if I had a satisfactory answer to one more question—

Lugath spoke angrily before I could frame it. "Why stand here gossiping with Mallin? Didn't you hear me? The Centaurs may be getting ready to lift the kid off Mars this moment, and years of work are going to waste! If Housk got as close to the truth as interrogating Mallin—it's a miracle he didn't reach any of my officers who were better informed, but I told them to keep out of sight, and so far . . . In any case, as I said the other night when you wanted to be open with Mallin, I'm not happy about him either! He turned up entirely too patly on Durrith. We may have kept our secrets well from the Centaurs, but Earthsiders are too damned sympathetic to the Bears, and Earth is the place where it's most difficult to keep the long-term plan from—"

I said, "Who are Peter Nizam and Lilith Choy?"

Lugath, interrupted, lost track of what he was saying. Thoder answered crisply. "Two extremely prominent young members of the pro-Bear faction on Earth, who have been agitating for a rift between the Old System and the Centaurs and a permanent alliance with the Bears."

"What would they be likely to do with the baby?"

Lugath and Thoder exchanged bewildered glances. Thoder said, "Deliver him to the Bears, naturally. And that would be a disaster second only to his remaining among Centaurs, to have his mind straitjacketed for life. Even if they could keep from boasting about their own cleverness—which I doubt, and which would quite possibly result in war—if that boy grows up pro-Centaur or pro-Bear rather than pro-mankind it would ruin the pattern of growth which the most selfless and dedicated planners of all time have evolved for us."

"And," I said, "what is all this to do with *you?*"

There was a silence. At length Thoder gave a shrug. "Since you know so much already, I might as well confess the rest. The quarterings you didn't recognise on the arms I showed you—the ones which don't belong to Tyrant Basil—are those of my own family. That very remarkable person, his mother, is my grand-daughter Shilene."

XV

STILL I HESITATED. When finally I chose sides for good and all, for better or worse, it wasn't for any selfless, dedicated reason. Not really.

Oh, there was some element of sympathy at the back of my mind. I could think of the Thoder I'd known as teacher-parent, recognise how much he loved children, imagine what it had cost him to part from his own—for never till this moment had I even suspected he might be a father—yet the idea remained remote, detached from me here and now.

On the other hand . . .

I hadn't had a chance, and would have had to retreat into extended time in order to get the chance, to consider and analyse what he'd told me about Centaurs and Bears. It all made sense at first glance—why, I myself had intuitively realised that from the very beginning of interstellar colonisation the Bear archetype must have looked northwards from the Old System, the Centaur archetype southwards, and this was hardly likely to be an accident.

Nonetheless, of three fates open before a child of such superlative genetic endowment as the one he'd described—not counting death or injury during this ridiculous undercover squabble over him—was I automatically to opt for what Thoder wanted? Was I convinced that it was in his, our, everybody's best interests that the baby should take the kind of pathway into life that I'd done? I'd more or less rejected Thoder's guidance, even if I'd wandered back into touch with him as a result of circumstances. Hadn't he barely finished telling me himself that the Martian way of life was an abandoned deadend, an alley pointing towards the future but leading nowhere, as obsolete as plans for a multigeneration interstellar ark on the day they tested the four-space driver?

I'd agree instantly that to return the baby to Centaur care would be to straitjacket his mind. But to let the Bears raise him didn't strike me as so alarming. Wild declarations of the risk of war following Bear boasting about their cleverness—this was a dreadful exaggeration. You just couldn't contemplate wars between the stars. The resources involved in mounting one would ruin the party who tried it, and the Centaurs' own worshipped computers would say so unequivocally.

Even if I were wrong, even if some astonishing new breakthrough proved that it was possible to have that war, the random hammering their society would receive would outrun Centaur capacity to adjust, while Bears—flexible, free and easy—would pick up the pieces and make do. The Old System would probably be pulverised, in Thoder's own simile like a grain of wheat between gigantic millstones. But what now did it boast worth keeping? Earthsiders had abdicated the crown of history in favour of the subjects of a monstrous laboratory experiment; as for Mars, it was a vermiform appendix serving no purpose any longer.

Peter and Lilith had been kind to me: not only saved my life, but dealt with me as a person and appealed to my Martian honour. They hadn't fully understood its implications, but at least they'd recognised its existence. Housk and his companions had treated me as a thing, to be squeezed with a nerve-whip until the juice of my knowledge trickled out. In Centaur space, for doing little more than speak my mind, I'd been discarded like an out-of-tolerance spare part. In Bear space I'd served with people I could call my friends, loved girls who thought of me as *me*, not simply "gangling giant" . . . Hell, I'd considered marrying one of them!

So the selfless conclusion, when the scales were charged on both sides, was—better the Bears. But I didn't come to it. I came to the selfish conclusion.

I could not stand to think that everything I prized, everything I'd lived by, should be scrapped, that the very concept "Martian" should be a hollow drum, noisy and empty. And if there was no longer any hope of building on a Martian basis towards a grand future for mankind, then at least let traces of what I valued survive in the memory of a child who would shake the stars when he grew to adulthood. It was not and could never be enough that genes were transmitted. Set a boy and a girl on a new world, perfectly fit for their survival—when they bred, could you call their children human beings in anything but shape? What made me a man wasn't in a sticky fluid crawling with whip-tailed monozygote cells. You couldn't centrifuge it, radiate it, modify it with multagenic compounds and set it under a microscope.

But it wasn't intangible, either. It wasn't beyond control, and most of all it wasn't inaccessible to the operation of man's greatest single gift: the talent of binding time over millions of years. You could plan to direct it. You could choose one part of it over another as bestowing a higher chance of survival. You could look at it long and soberly and say at last, "As far as I, here and now and admitting ignorance, can tell: that is bad and this is good."

I said, "They had the baby at Grand Canal Apartments a few hours ago, and a Bear came to collect him."

The moment after I'd made the announcement, a reason sprang to mind why it could not possibly be correct. The trip home to the Old System from Durrith had taken almost two months, even with Lugath's improbably powerful drivers, yet the child I'd heard crying at Peter and Lilith's had sounded very young indeed, and certainly no more than two weeks old, if as much.

That left me completely at a loss. Seconds ticked away during which both Thoder and Lugath demanded how I knew, until at last I amended my statement weakly.

"Or rather . . . there was *a* baby there, because I heard it crying. But it must have been much too young."

"Too young?" Lugath echoed. "Did you see it? No? Then —"

"Hearing is enough," Thoder told him curtly. "But hold on. Lugath, how was the baby transported? In a ship like yours, with limited passenger accommodation, there must have been some risk of his crying being overheard."

"Of course not! We contracted him. As far as he was concerned the voyage lasted only a matter of an hour or two."

"I don't quite—" Thoder began.

I broke in. "Then it *could* have been the same baby I heard at Peter and Lilith's!" And for Thoder's benefit, I amplified: "What Captain Lugath means is that though the baby was travelling with the ship he wasn't in the same four-spatial mode as the rest of it. He was in a mode very close to normal space and subject to relativistic time-contraction . . . Cosmos!"

"What's wrong?"

"No wonder I had so much trouble with those damned drivers! It's like—like trying to fly a fast aircraft with a ground-anchor catching in the rocks below!"

"Any time you want a recommendation from me," Lugath said soberly, "you can have it. My own engineer couldn't have made such fast time back to the Old System, and he knew about the special compartment in the alternate four-space mode."

"If you'd told *me*," I retorted, "I'd have got you here a week sooner!"

"Stop wrangling," Thoder sighed. "We assume it was the same baby you heard at Grand Canal Apartments. Tell us the rest—and describe the Bear who came to collect him."

I did so. Thoder snapped his fingers.

"Do you know him?" Lugath demanded.

"It sounds like a man called Jives, who enrolled at the College for a two-term course about—let me see—seven or eight weeks ago. I've been wondering about him ever since he arrived. He claims to be a manufacturer in a small way of business on Goldstar, but he checked out so high in the routine life-adjustment tests I was convinced he must be lying. His grades on personal power and social conformity were— Oh, to the Coalsack with the details! What counts is that I can swear to his being a Bear secret agent."

"Sent to cover the arrival of the baby?"

"Of course not, unless their espionage is fabulously efficient. No, more likely he was just ordered to enroll at the College and evaluate the effect it's having on the Bear students who form ninety-two per cent of the student body. Bears are sensitive about outside interference with the running of their society; they don't want any single influence to become dominant, and a few of our former graduates have done—let's say improbably well since they left Mars."

"Comweb!" Lugath said, and jumped to his feet.

We could hear him clearly through the flimsy wall of the adjacent room, but what he said was obviously linked to an association-code; only the agitated tone of his voice might have indicated to an outsider that his conversation about improved grades of nuclear fuel reflected something far deeper and more dangerous.

"Are you sure about this man Jives?" I asked Thoder.

He gave a sad bitter smile. "Still thinking that the post of a professor at the College of Serendipity is unworthy of an honest man? I assure you it's not. I instruct my class in the exercise of the skills which the ignorant describe as 'luck', and most of them are techniques you'd recognise from the mental games I used to make you play as a child. Stretching time, for example, to give extra opportunity for analysing a crisis situation—I still teach that in a play-context, but it's the Bears' favourite gambling games I use nowadays." He leaned forward.

"Much more must have happened to you today than simply overhearing a baby in Grand Canal Apartments. Tell me!"

Lugath had switched to another code now, and was talking about a complicated series of bets on a Bear athletics championship, the Zodiac Girdle Meet.

I summarised the path I'd taken to bring me back here.

"An ingenious notion to take advantage of Yuma's eidetic memory and short-cut your inquiries," he commented. "But I'm afraid you were lucky to learn even what little you did from him. I deliberately covered up my connections with the College of Heralds—you'll realise that if anyone were bright enough to wonder why heralds and luck-teachers were the two groups in the Old System currently exercising most influence over the great power-blocks he might stumble on what I've been telling you . . . And you found Housk in the room under the Temple, did you?"

"You know about it?"

"Oh yes. In fact I half-suspected that was where you'd been taken for your interrogation. I recognised the description of the stone chair; there are very few like it on Mars. It has alarming implications, incidentally, but they'll have to wait."

"What are they?"

"Mainly that the anti-Earthside sentiment common among Martians these days—witness yourself, if you'll forgive my being personal—must have turned sourer than I expected, if it's led to a Centaur being informed of that secret room. I imagined it was known only to a handful of native Martians."

I wanted to ask many more questions about that, but there was a far worse problem troubling me. I said, "What I don't understand is how in the galaxy you lost track of this child!"

"Paradoxical, isn't it? We bring off a coup at a distance of lightyears, organise one of the most flawless smuggling operations in history, and then we're laid low by what you identified as the basic drawback of being Martians.

"We dared not chance exposing that child to conditions which might harm his growth, especially the formation of his unique brain. Oyxgen lack doesn't affect a baby as badly as an embryo, but we'd already taken great risks by —by kidnapping him and shipping him as Lugath described. But we needed to absorb him into Martian society as quickly as we could, to distract the curious who might otherwise wonder about his origins.

"So we arranged to hide him in the perfect setting for a baby: a maternity clinic, with the borrowed identity of a child who failed to come to term and died before delivery. We thought we'd taken care of every eventuality; I simply didn't believe failure was possible. Yet we failed!

"In view of what you've told me, I'd bet that what wrecked our beautiful scheme was the fact that, as Martian maternity clinics have to be maintained at Earthside sea-level pressure, they are staffed by Earthside immigrants rather than Martians.

"Suppose a pro-Bear Earthsider on the clinic staff mentioned to a Bear friend—conceivably, Jives himself—that there was something suspicious about this baby. Noting the coincidence of timing between this and the *Hippodamia*, knowing from Peter Nizam that Centaurs were sufficiently interested in the ship's last voyage to do what they did to you, it would take no great mental agility to suspect a connection. As I said, an interest in genetics isn't confined to Centaurs with their love of heraldry. So far they can only suspect, but if they've made off with the baby their guesses must be perilously close to home!"

XVI

I STILL WANTED to learn how the baby had been taken from the clinic, but there was no point in asking Thoder— if he'd known, he'd have acted on the knowledge. In any case, we were interrupted by the return of Thoder, wiping his face.

"I'm having Jives checked on," he said. "And there'll be a watch kept on every Bear ship a-planet from now on. No Bear ship has applied for takeoff clearance before noon tomorrow, which is a mercy. If they knew what they'd got, they'd be hell-bent to get the boy out of Old System immediately."

He kicked a chair around, glowering at me. "And to think I imagined my part of the work was over when I docked!"

"What is your part of the work?" I asked.

He glanced at Thoder, who spread his hands. "Go ahead. Martian loyalty is the least negotiable kind there is."

"Well . . . There's a handful of ships—about fifteen in all—working in each direction out of Old System, which support an intelligence network. Man's a cagy and suspicious animal, and to direct the evolution of his society takes a great deal of information which neither Bears nor Centaurs will supply merely for the asking. Equally, Bears and Centaurs spy on one another, but I have the impression we're the most successful of the three operators. I once shipped two Bear agents off Mars—come to think of it, they were bound for Durrith—and I knew who they were but I don't believe they ever suspected us. So I notified the Centaur authorities, and a couple of times since then I've been given small confidential jobs to handle for them, on the basis of my proven trustworthiness . . ." He smiled without humour.

"Thoder!" he resumed. "If the worst comes to the worst, can we openly charge Jives with kidnapping?"

"The kid's Martian cover identity should be proof against local inquiries," Thoder answered. "Martians won't be inclined to inquire too closely into it, because—as witness Ray here—we're all so damned sensitive about the way we're treated nowadays."

"Set that as the line of retreat, then," Lugath said. "How about lines of advance?" He seemed almost to have forgotten my presence in the last few seconds. "Put on Kanaiken's shoes, will you?"

Instantly I recognised another of the games Thoder had drilled us through as children: "putting on so-and-so's shoes" meant thinking oneself into the place of the person named. I had no idea who Kanaiken might be, but I assumed from what Thoder now said that he must be Jives's superior, perhaps the local chief of Bear intelligence operations.

Add one to the long list of things I'd learned from Thoder as a mere piece of mental gymnastics, that now proved to have applications under truly deadly circumstances.

"Kanaiken!" Lugath said. "What do you know about the child?"

Thoder rubbed his chin thoughtfully. "We-ell . . . For some years past, possibly for as long as a generation, our people have been showing interest in Tyrant Boris's descendants, so we know that certain unusual genetic lines are being selected for in Centaur space. This is the subject to which the story I've been told most likely relates—"

"What story?"

"Too fast. I know that the Centaurs have been showing concern about a ship called the *Hippodamia*, one of their own. I probably know that this ties back to an engineer who fell sick on Durrith and was replaced by a Martian. I don't know what the Centaurs learned from the sick man, but educated guessing shows that it's either the cargo or the passengers which concern them, more likely than the crew. I dare not tackle the crew, since they're Centaurs, with the single exception of the replacement engineer. I most likely proceed on the assumption that a Martian serving aboard a Centaur ship is less sympathetic than most people in Old System towards the Bears. Accordingly I don't move to contact him directly, but invite the assistance of two Earth nationals with strong Bear sympathies: Peter Nizam and Lilith Choy."

"Do they learn anything?"

"Rather little, except that someone—probably the Centaur agents permanently stationed here—has become sufficiently worried to nerve-whip the Martian engineer, information that causes me to revise my estimate of the matter's importance upwards. Centaurs don't rattle easily, but this is panicky."

"Your guesstimate of what they're looking for?"

"A human target. At this stage, my primary assumption is a spy with valuable information."

"Do you have to modify this?"

"Rapidly. A pro-Bear employee of a maternity clinic reports suspicious circumstances surrounding a child of obviously non-Martian stock. The report reaches me through Jives, or another Bear agent, or perhaps Peter Nizam and Lilith Choy."

"What brings those two to Mars?"

"Discussions regarding pro-Bear activity on Earth. Anyway; the other thing besides a spy with important data which could so alarm the Centaurs would be the loss of an important genetic endowment which for some reason is not duplicable. Hypothesis: the illegitimate offspring of an outstanding line. I have endowment tests run at the clinic—basic ones which won't attract comment, not full-scale genotyping. The results suggest puerile genius. Hmmm! In this case my gamble in kidnapping the child is based on more than a hunch—on the need to carry out proper genetic examination."

"Therefore," Lugath said, "unless he's had access to private genotyping equipment he's not yet sure what he's got. Where's the best genotyping centre on Mars?"

"Pegasus. Which has the advantage of being far from Zond."

"Assume he sends a sample there. He won't get an answer until about midday tomorrow. Until then he'll be prepared to find his guesses are wrong."

"He's gambled too heavily. But I grant his rationalisation is most likely based on the hope of doing down the Centaurs rather than a positive gain for the Bears. Put on Grainger's shoes, will you? No, wait—first you must know what Ray did to Housk earlier today."

Thoder summed it up baldly, and Lugath absorbed the words with a succession of intent nods. At length he pantomimed drawing on shoes, and Thoder proceeded.

"What do you know for certain?"

"A man in delirium on Dorrith, engineer of the Centaur ship *Hippodamia,* has made incoherent references to the voyage he missed by falling ill. Larchman's disease . . . Typically, he'd have talked out his apprehensions about flying the ship with the special compartment in a variant four-space mode. The authorities would have been astute enough to get hold of an expert right away, and the expert would have deduced that the compartment held something small and living, probably a child. Uh—the sick man didn't know what child, but it would take only a little imagination to suggest a rich genetic endowment."

"Did you receive all this at one blow?"

"No, it came in two stages: a preliminary notification that something was odd about the ship on its last trip, and members of the crew should be located and interrogated, beginning with the Martian engineer who stood in for the sick man because the captain and his officers had previously been regarded as loyal and reliable. Then the news about the special compartment and its likeliest contents followed when the peak of delirium was past and the phase of talking out anxieties set in. Major and multiple revision of previous assumptions, especially the conclusion that the Martian knew nothing of the secret."

"Next step?"

"Hunting down the crew, up to and including the captain." Lugath took off his shoes for a moment. "By the way, I learn that a party from the ship-registration department of the Centaur embassy took over *Hippo* this afternoon. They seem to be searching her. I'm afraid it's a foregone conclusion that they'll take us for Bear agents; I shall have to apply for asylum on Earth. But the loss of one ship in our employ is a small price for a coup of this magnitude."

"If we bring it off," Thoder said sourly. "So the situation stands like this. Kanaiken knows he has a child in whose whereabouts the Centaurs are disproportionately interested; he suspects a key-line genius, but he won't have this confirmed until genotyping is complete, and he'll have to have that done commercially. If he's right, he'll want to avoid rumours getting back here. Pegasus is a good long way away."

"Moreover," Lugath said, "they tell me there's almost as much pro-Bear sentiment there as there is in Zond. Right?"

"Quite right. When he gets the report, Kanaiken will want to shift that child off Mars before gossip from Pegasus catches up with him. If he loses the baby before receiving the report, and then receives a *false* report indicating that the

Centaurs were panicking without adequate reason, he may not take steps to try and retrieve him."

"Slim chance, but our best hope. We shall have to feed him data to indicate a high-ranking Centaur genealogy but with no special talent."

"I can arrange to have such a genotype prepared easily enough. I even have an idea as to how we can engineer the substitution. As to Grainger, though: since your crewman didn't know the child's identity, all he can be flying by is the belief that it's a Centaur child. Can we mislead him into thinking that this is not after all the case?"

Lugath shook his head. "I'll have to think about that," he muttered. "Right now I'm going back on the comweb to see what I can find out at the genotype centres where I know people . . ."

Thoder sat for a long time in silence. "What a mess!" he said finally. "It's making everything consistent that's the difficulty. Easy enough to mislead Kanaiken into accepting that the child is high-rank Centaur but not otherwise very notable—provided we can find out where he's having the genotype done and slip in in time to ensure that it's looked after by someone we know."

"Is that not difficult?" I said.

"Cosmos, not especially! Wouldn't you expect the majority of the people who know about the long-term plan to be in just such jobs as staffing a genotype centre?"

"Of course," I muttered. "Who's Kanaiken, by the way?"

"Local head of Bear intelligence. And Grainger is his Centaur counterpart. Who more than likely thinks that he's facing a coup by Bears, not by us—Lugath's ship is always carefully sown with misleading clues to direct attention away from the truth, he tells me. So we have to adapt our attempts to fool Kanaiken in such a way as to satisfy him that the Centaurs were panicking over nothing, while making Grainger believe that the Bears' alleged coup misfired. We must lure him into the assumption that—"

Lugath re-entered the room briskly. "Correct on the first try!" he said. "I spoke to Yetta Dryfoos at Pegasus, and she knew at once what I was talking about. Jives called her under his own name about two hours ago to ask how long it would take to run the test. She told him to get the material on the next available flight and, as Pegasus time is out of phase with ours in Zond, she could return it to him by noon tomorrow—exactly my estimate."

"That's our first stroke of luck today, apart from having Ray turn up," Thoder said. "I'm glad none of my pupils at the College of Serendipity is within earshot. Did she ask what we wanted to interfere for?"

"I thought it better not to tell her, and she agreed," Lugath shrugged. "In fact, what she wants is to be given the misleading material exactly as if it were the sample from Jives, and test it instead; that way, even she won't know what the true sample implies. She said she'd rather remain in the dark about it."

"Ray," Thoder murmured, "isn't your father in Pegasus at the moment? I heard from him a short time ago. He complained that you don't go and visit him any more."

XVII

ONE OF MY EARLY instructors in space-drive theory used to make great play with the paradoxical point that it was essentially more trouble to fly from Zond to Pegasus than from Earth to Mars. True, and a source of discouragement when it came to calling on people around the back of the planet. Our thin air—pressure at ground something like 100 on our standard scale of thousands of Earthside altitude-feet—was enough to be a nuisance but inadequate for economic winged flight. Freight transport was mainly by cushion-wheeled trucks such as one could see any day on the streets of Zond, but fast passenger transit was a tougher proposition. All kinds of ideas had been tried. Pure ballistic vehicles were out of the question, and so were ramjets. Oxygen being so scarce on Mars, any airbreathing vehicle had to carry its own oxidant at prohibitive cost, the same applying to rocket oxidants if the engines were used for more than the shortest possible part of the trip. Attempts to exploit the energy available from free radicals—lacking an ozone layer as we did, sunlight generated a lot of these—had proved abortive, and the eventual semi-solution was a kind of re-entry vehicle boosted to sub-orbital height and then skimmed in a series of hops to the destination with variable-aspect wings. They were uncomfortable, hence unpopular, and I'd never seen one with a full complement of passengers.

I didn't this time. But as I was stowing my gear in the elastic net of the baggage-sling over my seat, I discovered that this particular ship was overcrowded.

It contained, to my dismay, Major Housk.

What in the galaxy was he doing here? I was instantly ready to slip away and take a later flight, even if it meant Jives wouldn't get his report from Pegasus at the time promised; better to risk his unfounded suspicions of interference than hint to Housk that I was deeper involved—

Too late. He'd spotted me, and was approaching with determined strides. His face was flushed and his pupils dilated, facts that reinforced my dismay, for they indicated he'd taken one of the Centaur stimulants, most likely one of the high-order amphetamine derivatives.

I decided to salve what initiative I could and launch a frontal attack. "Not busted to the ranks yet?" I said in my most insulting voice, forestalling his own first words.

The gibe went home, but he didn't rise to it. "Going to Pegasus!" he grunted, pointing at the labels on my bags.

"If my father weren't expecting me to be on this flight," I said, "I'd call the police and lay an information against you for what you did to me the other night."

He gave a harsh laugh. "What I did to you? You're a fool, aren't you? Basing an accusation on something I said while you were nerve-whipping me would be futile. Anyway, don't you Martians dislike the police here because they're an Earthside and not a Martian institution?"

Which was penetratingly accurate; I was reminded of Peter and Lilith referring to the same point. But I felt I should continue trying to rile him—it was safe to do so, since it was consistent with the reaction of a merely angry man.

"I presume someone found you under the Old Temple," I muttered. "A shame. I hoped it would be the smell of your body rotting which finally attracted attention."

"I was found by someone in no position to take action against me," he snapped. "So your hope of seeing me busted in rank has gone phut, hear me? Instead I expect to come out of this with a commendation or two!"

I added another to the list of distinctions one could make between Centaur and Bear culture: Centaurs were shame-oriented and didn't basically care what they did provided they could do it without others finding out and their social standing being undermined, whereas Bears constituted a guilt-culture and carried their own moral standards around in their consciences.

What counted now, though, was that he sounded triumphant. I must try and get him to boast further, cluing me in on the way he thought he'd turned the tables. I was casting around for another line of attack when the takeoff warning sounded and I lost my chance, for with a final scowl he obeyed the warning like a good Centaur and turned to resume his own seat up front.

What could have made him so cocky? I wrestled with that problem all the way to Pegasus. In the end I resolved that I had better watch him after landing and try to see where he was headed.

He was too alert to give me the opportunity, though, and deliberately hung about until I could not convincingly miss any more cabs. I sighed and called one, instructing it to start off in the direction consistent with my statement that my father was expecting me. My last sight of Housk suggested that he was making for a public comweb—to verify that my father actually lived here, most probably.

I had no intention of going straight to my father's lodgings. Tucked in an inner pocket I was carrying a small sample of tissue: not artificial, which would have been both extremely expensive and too likely to be faulty, but modified to convey exactly the idea Thoder had mentioned—that the donor was from a high-ranking Centaur bloodline but had inherited no truly remarkable combination of genes.

That sample I had to deliver as soon as possible to the woman Lugath had contacted: Yetta Dryfoos. She was on the staff of the Pegasus maternity clinic—as everywhere, geno-typing and maternity went together on Mars. Only Centaurs carried the planning of their descendants to such lengths, but it was a human habit for parents to wonder about what they were going to have to bring up.

I gave the cab the appropriate revised instructions.

When I was shown into her glass-ceilinged office, the cleanest, lightest and most spacious room I'd seen on Mars for a long time, I stopped dead. She was so much of a rarity that since I'd been travelling to other worlds I'd almost convinced myself women like her didn't exist, and my youthful impression that they did was due to lack of adult discrimination.

She was both multi-generation Martian, and beautiful.

She rose to greet me, revealing that she stood about sixten. Black straight hair hung to her shoulders, framing a face longer than oval, with a broad forehead, high cheekbones, a firm, slightly thin-lipped mouth. Her complexion was a warm copper-brown. She wore a loose coverall of satiny white fabric that tended to mask the curves of her body, but it was clear nonetheless that she had the true proportions of her height. Like me, virtually all Martians were lean, and some would say lanky, but she was slender, a term that came belatedly to mind because so few of our women deserved it.

"Miss Dryfoos?" I said, and found I was laying an imperceptible private stress on the former word.

She smiled, showing magnificent white teeth. "You've made excellent time! My uncle warned me that you—ah—your package might not be ready in time for you to catch so early a flight."

"Your uncle?"

"Why, yes—your former teacher, I understand."

I shook my head in bewilderment. "I thought you were a friend of Captain Lugath's. I didn't know you were kin to Thoder."

"The captain may not know, either. My uncle is discreet about his relatives, because by no means all of us have led such retiring lives."

I was going to have to investigate Thoder's family. I was coming around to the idea that they must exercise enormous influence in Martian affairs. And come to think of it: why not? Mars's sparse population meant that one outstanding heredity-line would literally stand out more than on a crowded Earth-type world, just as we spoke of a mountain and meant hills a few hundred feet high, rare on Mars.

Perhaps Thoder's family reflected in little what they were hoping to do with the Centaur-Martian line represented by his great-grandson—

"What shall I do with the sample Jives sent?" She had opened a drawer in a wall-hung cabinet.

"Destroy it," I said promptly. "Run your tests on this one instead." I handed her the faked sample, which she slid into the drawer before carrying the real one to a disposall shute next to the door.

"Good," she said, dusting her hands. "Now it won't be a complete deception; Jives will get his report in exactly the same terms as he'd have got anyway. Thank you. Without knowing what this is all about, but having great respect for my uncle, I'm sure you've done an important service."

Was that going to be all? Apparently, for she was returning to her desk, and asking: "Can you find your own way out?"

Too much was at stake to waste time in casual chat. Yet I felt a stab of disappointment. Having chanced on a lovely woman like this, at the very least I wanted to *look* at her!

A fact that she recognised with disconcerting candour. For she gave me a twinkling smile.

"Forgive me saying this, won't you? But the only Martian men who ever come in this room as strangers, then walk out again—ah—hovering a little, are uninterested in women generally. I appreciate it. It's very flattering. But I have a hell of a lot of time to make up if I'm going to meet the deadline I promised Jives without realising anything odd was going on."

I gave an embarrassed grin and went out.

The corridors and hallways of the building were empty. The Martian staff, happy in this area pressurised to 10, were of course in the minority; most of the people who worked here must be on the maternity side behind airlocks in a thick clammy Earthside atmosphere. Damn this necessity which still tied us to Earth like an umbilical cord!

I saw no one else at all, therefore—not even the young man who'd shown me into Yetta Dryfoos's presence (and *that* was a better way of putting it than simply "into her office") while I was leaving. On the path connecting the building to the sidewalks of the town, I met a man with the general air of a husband coming to call on his wife in the pressurised maternity clinic, carrying sandflowers and a box of apples; then two porters, Earthside immigrants, humping cases of medical supplies with alarming ease in the low gravity. I walked absently for a considerable distance, my mind occupied with a picture of Yetta Dryfoos, until it occurred to me that I ought to work out where I was going.

Unlike Zond, a canal-town spreading along the floor of a rift valley for the sake of the natural enclosure it formed, Pegasus was a crater-town, bowl-shaped, with its main thoroughfares arranged like a Shield of David. I had just calculated that if I walked to my father's lodgings I ought to arrive about in time for the midday meal, when I saw the cab go past on the dusty street outside.

Its passenger was a man I'd have recognised anywhere. And there was only one place in the direction he was heading where he was likely to be bound for.

I spun around and began to race after him with all the speed my loping Martian gait could afford.

Of course, the cab had dropped him and gone long before I reached the entrance of the genotype centre again. I dashed into the hallway, almost bowling over an elderly woman carrying a rack of solido gene-models, and stormed towards the office I'd left a few minutes before.

I opened its door silently, silently, blessing the standard of Martian honour which made even the provision of locks on doors superfluous, for certainly Housk would have locked intruders out if he could. There he was, levelling his beloved nerve-whip at Yetta, rasping orders to her that she should get out and give him the tissue-sample she'd received from Jives.

So the Centaurs knew far more about what was going on than Thoder had imagined. But there was no time to worry about that. I had to act before the rounding of Yetta's eyes, their involuntary shift of focus, gave me away.

I managed it. I had to be brutal, but I was weak compared to anyone raised on a one-gee planet. I clamped my hand over Housk's eyes and hauled him backwards to stumble on my outstretched leg. I don't think he had been more surprised even when I took the whip away from him in the room under the Old Temple. He yelled and crashed to the floor with a thump, and Yetta dodged around her desk to snatch at his whip. Somehow we twisted it loose from his frantic grasp, and she leaped back out of his reach with movements as fluid and graceful as a dance.

"Thank you," she said when she had recovered her normal calm. "And now can you tell me who the hell he *is*?"

XVIII

IT WOULD HAVE been comical, if it hadn't been so pathetic, to watch Housk's hope of emerging from this tangle evaporate from his face. It carried away with it all his colour, leaving him pasty-pale, and all the spurious bravado lent by the stimulants he'd taken.

But there was no time to explain the background to Yetta. The crash with which he had slumped to the floor had resounded through this entire building. The first person to come inquiring was the elderly woman I'd almost bumped into as I rushed to the rescue, but she was joined within another few seconds by half a dozen startled members of the staff, half of them Earthsiders.

Among them was an authoritative man of late middle age, hair a shock of iron-grey, who instantly assumed charge of the nerve-whip: a Martian, fortunately.

Lacking guidance, the only thing Yetta could do was pretend ignorance. "Thank you, Dr Snell," she said. "I think the man must be crazy. He came charging in here without warning, drew his whip, and ordered me to give him the contents of the tissue-sample cupboard. If I hadn't been saved by Mr Mallin—"

"And what brought you here?" Snell inquired of me.

"I'm from Zond, where Yetta's uncle lives," I said. "I'm in Pegasus to visit my father, and I was asked to bring her a message while I was here."

"Lucky you turned up." Snell gestured to his colleagues. "Well, better get him on his feet and put him somewhere safe until the police arrive."

"It's all lies!" Housk blasted. "You damned Martians are born lying! Mallin knows perfectly well who I am and why I'm here—why don't you ask him about the child he kidnapped?"

"Child? What child?" Snell blinked.

"Oh!" Yetta chimed in loudly. "Maybe that would explain his behaviour. Are you suffering from the delusion that he kidnapped your child? Did you come here to look for it?" She winked enormously at Snell, intending that Housk should see it.

"No, you can't get away with that," Housk thundered. "Are you in charge here? If you are, look through that cupboard and you'll find a Centaur tissue-sample—"

"I wouldn't be at all surprised," Snell shrugged. "As a matter of fact, we usually have two or three hundred Centaur tissue-samples—"

"I mean the one that was sent to you by a man called Jives!"

"Doctor, we're on the fringe of a paranoid fantasy, I think," Yetta murmured. "I have such a sample, but Jives is a Bear citizen, I believe—he has a Bear accent, anyway!"

Housk must have read Snell's agreement with the suggestion from his expression. All at once he seemed to slump. He spoke again in a changed voice: thick, slow, hopeless.

"Lies, nothing but lies from start to finish. This is a planet of maniacs living in a dream. I should have known when we found out about the Old Temple."

"What was that?" I said. I couldn't help myself.

He recovered a part of his poise and sneered at me. "Oh, yes—you know about the Temple, don't you? Or you think you do! You whipped me unconscious and left me there, didn't you? And if Raglan hadn't found me and told me about Jives, you'd have got away with it. But you're not going to, I swear you're not!"

Snell looked at me. I shook my head, and after a second of private debate he decided to take my word over that of a Centaur who'd broken in and threatened Yetta with his whip. He motioned that Housk should be led away.

"Not so fast!" Housk freed himself with a jerk of both arms and took the pace needed to confront me. "Dirty

Martian scum—shall I tell you about your precious Temple? We know more about it than you do! Why, we've used that room where you whipped me for years and years and years, and nobody but us ever goes there. Blockhead! How many times have you stood gaping at those famous fifteen arte-facts, and never once bothered to ask what they're doing in a display case instead of being analysed and studied and replicas being put on show instead of the real thing?"

The Earthsiders in the room exchanged worried glances, but this was something any Martian would want to know about.

"Fakes!" Housk crowed. "That's what they are—fakes, planted to make people believe in aboriginal Martians! We've known the truth for years. Who but stupid Martians would have fallen for a simple hoax? If there were ever *real* Martians, or if there were visitors from the stars who stopped over on Mars, we wanted to know about them, so we investigated, and we found the stones were dressed with tools having metric-system dimensions. *Men* built your stinking temple!" He was almost frothing, so eager was he to get back somehow at the Martians who'd frustrated his last des-perate hope of saving his reputation before his superiors found out how he'd bungled his responsibilities.

It was a fair bet that this man Raglan, who'd discovered him lying unconscious when bringing a report on Jives, must be a Centaur agent using the temple room as a mail-drop—precisely as I'd guessed. His interest in Jives could be due to nothing more remarkable than that the Centaurs sus-pected him, as Thoder did, of being a Bear agent. In view of the sensitive location of the Old System between the two blocs, each side would want to watch the other closely.

It followed with high probability that Housk had told no one else of his new data. He'd seized on the chance to steal the tissue-sample and get it to his chief, Grainger, as insurance against the consequences of letting himself be overpowered and questioned by me. From this, further im-plications fanned out. I didn't bother tracing them all, but seized on the first that offered to be helpful.

I said, "I thought all Centaurs knew about Plato."

"What?" Sensing that his bombshell wasn't working, he peered up at me.

"Never heard of a 'noble lie'?" Inwardly I was shaking; what he said about the Temple could be—almost certainly was—correct, and the most cherished of my surviving childhood illusions was blowing away like sand before the wind. But I wasn't going to let a mere Centaur see that!

"You're the child of a four-space driver, *little man,*" I said. "But my ancestors, *our* ancestors, our *Martian* ancestors, were quite prepared to go to the stars the hard way if they had to, in multi-generation ships like arks, dying billions of miles from home in the hope that their children's children would visit the stars! Don't you think it was a welcome reminder that the idea wasn't absurd, to have a big, mysterious, inexplicable building as concrete evidence, and strange incomprehensible things on display inside it?"

I looked at Yetta, and her eyes were shining. Fantastic. Even as I spoke, I had the sensation that what I was saying was true in some sense larger than ordinary facts—in the sense in which a myth is true.

"And," I said cruelly, "you fooled yourselves. Can you think of a worse place to use as a torture-chamber for a Martian than the very symbol of his most beloved traditions?"

He got that, all right. It must have seemed to him that I'd drawn strength from the surroundings of the Temple and resisted the worst he could do to me during his interrogation, whereas he'd succumbed at once when the tables were turned. Being shown so grossly weak by comparison with one of us despised Martians wrecked the last vestige of his self-control, and he was actually blubbering when he was taken away.

I took advantage of the interruption to ask Yetta softly how many of these people were trustworthy, and she told me that if I could convince Snell I could rely on him to get the rest of the staff to keep quiet, at least for a time. I took a detour into extended time to review the possibilities, and settled for a set of half-truths.

I told him enough to let him guess at a great deal more and add the whole up to an impressive total. I said I was back from a trip into Centaur space which had revealed the operations of Housk and his companions in a new light; they were trying to undo the prevalent pro-Bear sympathies of Earthsiders on Mars; I was ignorant of his purpose in asking for the tissue-sample, but it was probably an anti-Bear plot, and anyway what business did Centaurs *or* Bears have conducting their squabbles on Mars?

The final point went deep in his mind, and we had no trouble persuading him to ensure that the news went no further. He asked what I wanted to do with Housk—what I wanted! I could scarcely tell him, but it seemed safest to put him into police custody and let his Embassy reclaim him if and when they wanted to. Once his superiors learned what he'd been up to, especially when they learned that he had withheld Raglan's report instead of relaying it, he would be shipped home so fast he'd burn up from the friction.

Having got rid of Snell, I turned to Yetta. There was a pause.

"Did you—did you know about the Old Temple?" she said finally.

I shook my head.

"Then . . ."

"I made it up," I said savagely. "But I'm damned if I was going to let him get away with it!"

"You made it up." She turned the words over in imagination, and went on, "In that case, I think I rather like you. It was exactly what everyone needed to hear, especially myself. I don't know what in the world my uncle is getting up to at the moment, and I was so reluctant to think that I might be involved that I almost turned down Lugath's request to accept the tissue-sample you brought. I'd have said it was an insult to Martian integrity to cheat an offworlder by giving false information. But now—well, what has this man Jives done?"

"Kidnapped one of your relatives," I said, and in the same moment suddenly saw that Thoder had made a mistake.

Thoder! I wouldn't have believed it possible! But years of living his quiet, inconspicuous existence as a teacher, cut off even from his influential kinfolk, must have conditioned him into the habit of secrecy and non-involvement with public institutions.

"What?"

"Kidnapped one of your relatives!" It was an inspiration that had come to me. Why was Thoder wasting his time in this elaborate pattern of deceit, this absurd racing against time with only the resources available through friendship and shared secret knowledge? "What do you know about a girl called Shilene?"

Yetta's face hardened momentarily. The fleeting expression told me I was right. I seemed to have been able to step outside my own environment for the first time, make as clear an assessment of Martian society as I could of Bear or Centaur.

Our standards of honourable behaviour, instanced by my expressing obligation to Peter and Lilith for saving my life, by the fact that we didn't lock doors against fellow-Martians, weren't isolated in our culture any more than they had ever been. They were associated to form a coherent pattern, exemplified by my refusal to go on monumental sprees when I was at home, though I often did so elsewhere, and equally by my willingness to have casual affairs with Bear girls I didn't intend for a moment to marry, while reserving at the back of my mind a long-term vision of marrying on Mars. A double standard of classic quality! In short, our Martian culture was a stock puritanical pioneer one, with the same strengths and weaknesses as Puritan New England in the seventeenth century.

My flash of insight was confirmed by Yetta's reply to my question: "Shilene? How did you hear of her? We're not exactly proud of that branch of our family, you know!"

"You damned well ought to be," I said. "I've just learned that I'm not willing to sacrifice my Martian illusions that make me comfortable, while she must have sacrificed a hell of a lot more—almost as much as Thoder."

I was about to demand a comweb so I could contact Thoder and explain his mistake before we lost our chance to do more than salvage the situation—to turn it, indeed, into a spectacular triumph over both Bears and Centaurs. Then something Housk had said clicked in my mind. This unknown Raglan had told him about Jives and the delivery of the tissue-sample to this genotype centre, half around the planet from Zond. The only way such information could have leaked out was if the Centaurs were able to tap comwebs. Safer, then, to go back to Zond.

"Get out that tissue-sample I brought," I said to Yetta. "Don't argue. Jives won't need a test run on it by the time we've finished with him. Collect the absolute minimum of belongings and come with me."

"But you must explain!" she said, looking vaguely frightened.

"Let your uncle explain," I snapped. "Come on—move!"

XIX

"THODER! THODER!"

I strode into the house shouting at the top of my lungs. Behind me Yetta stood uncertainly, eying the furniture and decorations.

A noise came from the room on my left. I swung around and reached for the handle to open its door. It opened fractionally sooner, and there was—not Thoder, but Lugath.

"Mallin!" he barked, and would have gone on but that he glanced past me and recognised Yetta. His air had been of mere tiredness and harassment when he emerged; abruptly it changed to fury.

"Cosmos! What are you doing here? Have you brought that genotype for Jives? There'll be hell to pay if he doesn't get it as promised."

"He's not getting it," she said.

"What?" Lugath's face went grey. "But—"

"A Centaur who seems to be some kind of a spy turned up and demanded that I give him the tissue-sample," Yetta sighed. "Beyond this, you'll have to ask Ray."

Lugath rounded on me. "Housk?" he breathed, scarcely crediting his own suspicion.

"Yes, Housk. He didn't get away with it—I interfered. But it doesn't make a sliver of difference."

"Are you crazy?" Lugath's voice peaked towards frenzy. "Did you cover up?"

"We handed him over to the Pegasus police, and I guess he'll get back to their Embassy some time."

"Oh, no." Lugath put both hands to his head. "What a

brilliant idea. That's all we need. I suppose lots and lots of people in Pegasus have been told all about it, too!"

"Well, it was hard to keep quiet when six or seven people came to see what the trouble was, and found Housk on the floor and Yetta standing over him with a nerve-whip."

Lugath felt wordlessly for support, and leaned heavily on the nearest wall. "So that's it," he said emptily. "It's gone for nothing, and there won't be another chance like it for generations."

"Wrong," I said. "It's the best thing that could possibly have happened, because it let some daylight into the whole confused business."

"You must be out of your mind," Lugath said. "When Jives doesn't get the tissue-sample, and makes inquiries, and hears about this intrusive Centaur, he'll realise—"

"Hold on! You're still skulking around in your maze of secrecy, Lugath, and the time for that is over. This is Mars, remember? Not Leovang or Durrith or anywhere else, but Mars!"

I looked in vain for a sign of comprehension from him, but too many years spent among Centaurs, passing as one himself, had put up the shutters around his mind. Anyhow, it wasn't Lugath I wanted to convince of my inspiration, but Thoder.

"Where is Thoder?" I demanded.

"Where do you think he is?" Lugath responded wearily. "At the College of Serendipity?"

"Of course. He works there, so he has every right to be at the place, and our best estimate of the whereabouts of the baby is that he's in Jives's possession, and Jives is ostensibly a student at the college."

"Yetta! Go look for a cab with cross-country wheels. We have to get about five miles out of town, and quickly!"

"Mallin, you'll make things ten times worse if you go blasting in with all jets. All it would take is one unaccountable action to—"

"For pity's sake!" I exploded. I took from my pocket the faked tissue-sample which had proved so unnecessary and waved it under Lugath's nose. "There are three things which are extraordinary about that baby, not two! Sure he's Centaur, and sure he's a potential prodigy—but on top of that he's also part-Martian, and if you don't see what's important about that I'm damned certain Thoder will!"

"Cab coming," Yetta reported from the doorway.

The route from here to the College of Serendipity was along the hairpinned road near Grand Canal Apartments. It was incredibly frustrating to have to cover five times the straightline distance simply because we had to reach mainsurface from the bottom of the canal. I sat tensely forward on my seat, glowering through the dust which the vehicle kicked up.

"Hell," I muttered, "I could get up this slope faster on foot!"

Yetta didn't answer directly. When we had rounded another bend, though, she said, "Ray, are you sure you know what you're doing? Lugath seemed terribly—"

"Lugath is trapped in a mental maze, the same as I was," I said. "He's spent far too long pretending he's a Centaur."

"Even so—"

"Yetta, please! No, I'm not sure I know what I'm doing, only ninety per cent convinced of the idea. But between here and the place we're going I think I can take care of the other ten per cent—if you'll let me concentrate."

"I'm sorry." She pressed her lips together and sat back.

Right. Now I had the broad outlines of the story I wanted to make Thoder accept, so—

The cab reached mainsurface level and swung past the penthouse of Grand Canal Apartments, and at that very instant a figure emerged from the doorway. Masked, muffled in warm outdoor clothing, even so nothing could have prevented me from recognising the diminutive stature of Lilith Choy, nor her from recognising me hunched forward as I was close to the windshield of the cab and staring out.

She was standing stock still as we passed her. Glancing back, I saw with a heart-dropping pang that she had immediately started to re-enter the apartment.

In this direction, there was one possible destination only: the college. The road led nowhere else. Indeed, it was a mere track. Did they know of a link between me and Thoder, or between me and Jives? It wasn't yet time for the delivery of the promised genotype report, but even so . . .

To hell with it. I strained my eyes to see whether there was another vehicle following us, but I saw none, and anyhow it would have meant nothing if I had done—the college was popular with the most improbable people, not only Bears.

I'd never actually seen the place. It was about as weird as I'd imagined before I learned that Thoder was lecturing at it; since then, my mental picture had been toned down to comparative respectability.

Actually, it was almost funny. Like most isolated Martian structures, it consisted in a series of domes connected by pressurised walkways, but this underlying conventionality was completely obscured by the decorations. They began with a larger-than-life group of statues—inevitably, Apprehension, Hope and Certainty, the classic Bear symbols—in gilded ugliness above the main gate from the road. They continued in a welter of phantasmagoric allusions: luck-symbols from every planet where such a concept was recognised loomed on all sides. One dome was painted as a gameboard, another as a deck of cards; a lightning-conductor jutted up from another still, as absurd as the bit of red thread sometimes tied around a baby's wrist on Earth, to strengthen the joint and protect against rheumatism, for there had never been a thunderstorm on Mars!

Some other time I'd look over this grand array of nonsense and have myself a good laugh. Right now, I was in a hurry. The cab halted at the main entrance of the college. I took Yetta's hand and led her at a dead run inside the building.

The college had the noisy silence characteristic of every educational institution I'd ever been in, orthodox or crank, composed of the resonance of many voices distant along echoing passageways. There was no one in sight. Swallowing hard to adjust to the pressure here—kept up to four for the benefit of the Bear majority among the students—we hastened along the entrance corridor until we came to a sort of assembly hall from which at least six others diverged.

"Hell! Which way?" I snapped.

Yetta pointed. "There's a bulletin board!"

I strode over to it. Scanning the details posted for the

students, I found such choice chunks of crankery as *Harmony II, Adjustment to Planetary Rhythms,* and *Open Lecture: The Influence of Temperature and Humidity on Cross-Complex Luck Nexi,* interspersed with sensible-sounding subjects such as probability in its application to card-games.

Ah: *Life-Adjustment,* a course of six lectures by Professor (Emeritus) Thoder. I ran a finger down the table of dates and times, located today, and found that the lecture was being given in the Central Demonstration Hall.

I hunted everywhere for signs, or a plan of the college. Finding none, I called to Yetta.

"We'll just have to hope that luck is freely available here! Let's try the biggest corridor first."

She nodded and came towards me. A door leading on to the hall opened abruptly with a creak of complaint, and a woman peered out.

She looked like a child's comic doll. She stood about as high as Yetta's elbow, but added to this with the help of an immense coiffure, stacked and stacked in several layers each of a different colour: white, yellow, brownish-red, brown and black. Cosmetics made her face an ageless mask, which might have belonged to a child pretending to be an adult or an elderly woman persuading herself she was still young. Purple-irised eyes like holes in the mask fixed us.

"According to Hucker," she said in a voice that screaked almost as agonisingly as the door, "you've just set yourself back at least a hundred turns on the spiral of the Greatest Game."

"What?" I blinked foolishly at her, decided that her aid was better than nothing, and pursued the important subject. "Look, where's the Demonstration Hall, where Professor Thoder is lecturing?"

"Oh, I couldn't possibly let you go in there after what you just said," she answered with a headshake so violent I thought it would dislodge her piled-up hair. "You did say, didn't you, that luck was 'freely available'? One mustn't even think this. Please go before your auras disturb the general harmony of the institution."

She advanced on me, waving both arms as though shooing away an annoying small animal.

"Where's the Demonstration Hall?" I repeated.

"Go away. Go *away*. Who let you in, anyhow? We always have to screen our disciples most thoroughly, and as a result this is a focus of universal harmonies unparalleled in the galaxy. Coming in here in your state of mind is like—like shovelling sand into a watch!"

"Have you taken any of Thoder's lectures?"

"What? Goodness, no. He teaches only the visiting students, not the resident staff."

"I thought not. Thoder would knock that nonsense out of you fast enough. But since he's not here I'll have to do." I bunched my fist and waved it under her nose. "Do you tell me where to find him, or shall I kick you in the aura?"

"Help," she said in a thin voice, and looked appealingly at Yetta.

Yetta folded both arms on her handsome bosom and looked down with tall Martian scorn. She said, "What happens if we find it by good old trial and error, hmmm?"

Clever girl! I should have thought of that. The woman with the dreadful hair uttered a sigh of horror, and I thought she was going to give in, but at that moment a gong chimed softly, and there was a redoubling of the background noise: the end-of-class explosion common to any school.

"Professor Thoder will pass us on his way out," she said. "And when he gets here, I'll give him a piece of my mind."

"Have you any to spare, really?" Yetta said with superbly insulting sweetness. I forgot everything else, though. Craning on tip-toe over the heads of the students who now washed down the corridors from all directions, I tried to spot Thoder—yes, there he was, looking tired and dispirited.

In the instant he saw me, I took a deep breath. He wasn't going to like my doing this, but I could save valuable time by making him build on a *fait accompli* rather than persuading him to fall in with my plan instead of his.

"Thoder!" I shouted, for everyone to hear. "Your great-grandson is here! It's definite now—it *is* him!"

He looked as if he couldn't believe his ears. Dismay and and alarm crossed his face, and then he came charging towards me, ordering students out of his way, to seize my arm

and demand in a frantic whisper the same thing Lugath
had asked: was I out of my mind?

"No," I said. "In it, for the first time in my whole life.
Where can we go to talk quietly?"

XX

As I LAID BARE the flaw in Thoder's original assumptions,
I could feel all around us the rapid percolation of what
I'd shouted in the hall. It would be picked up and re-
layed in puzzled tones by Thoder's own students, who might
think they knew him and were surprised to discover he had
relatives; it would travel likewise for its own sake—an
unexpected event intruding—among those who didn't know
him: "Some crazy Martian came shouting along the corridor, something about Prof Thoder's grandson, or something
. . ."

Being Thoder, the old man disciplined himself into listen-
ing. That, though, didn't last long. So swiftly that I was
taken aback, he saw through my own confused explanations
to the heart of the matter.

"Let me confirm that I've understood properly," he re-
quested. "You are saying that the need for secrecy and
elaborate cover stories ceased the moment we successfully
landed the baby on Mars. We should according to you then
have taken the fuel from both Bear and Centaur jets by loudly advertising what we'd done.

"The published version of events would involve three
superficially convincing falsehoods. The first: that you, an
ex-pupil of my own, turned space-engineer, had been en-
listed in order to try and forestall a Bear coup. The second:
that such a coup existed, that Lugath's ship was acting for
Bears rather than for the Old System espionage network—as
witness the misleading clues which the Centaurs will have
found when they inspected it—and that his action in re-
porting two Bear agents to the Centaur authorities was a
cover designed to make those authorities think he was
perfectly loyal. And the third: that I have disowned my
granddaughter Shilene." His eyes were large with sadness,
but none of it coloured his voice.

"You would rely for the success and public acceptance of this story on three sociological assumptions. As regards the Bears, you feel that they would be content to withdraw from their involvement. It would be a blow to pro-Bear sentiment in this system if they claimed that they in fact did plan to kidnap the baby, but conversely it would suit them well to have the Centaurs believe their espionage was so brilliant they knew about the child; you'd expect them to issue a formal disclaimer of involvement couched in neutral terms that the Centaurs would disregard. As far as the Centaurs themselves are concerned, they will find it sufficient of a blow to have news of the Tyrant Presumptive's connection with a—a courtesan noised abroad. In the glare of such publicity, and moreover in the wake of the scandal which will follow Housk's ill-judged behaviour, they'll be compelled to swallow the existing situation without making further attempts to trace the child. Tyrant Basil will not wish to show excessive interest in an illegitimate grandson, for fear this might be interpreted as a gesture towards recognising him as a lineal successor, and you need only look at their obsession with heraldry to see how this would disrupt their standard procedures. Moreoever, the same habit will make it seem entirely logical to them that I, as an enraged grandparent, took steps to reclaim my descendant from the care of a girl whose life had been—ah—morally most irregular."

Still he could have been analysing an abstract problem.

"And the third support on which you rest your proposals is the way in which Yetta here reacted when you mentioned Shilene." His eyes flickered briefly to Yetta; she was stitting still as stone.

"You're absolutely right, Ray. Our society on Mars is a puritanical one. One doesn't think of that as being a term of praise, yet in some senses it is. How could our forefathers have envisaged the kind of rigid independent culture they wanted to develop here, as a foil and contrast to Earthside laxity and uniformity, had there not been such unbreakable standards as a puritan thought-pattern implies? Merely because we were overtaken by events, and our designed function was made obsolete by starflight, hasn't invalidated this underlying strictness. Let it only be said that I *am* an enraged grandparent, and every proud Martian will rally to my side against Bears, Centaurs and Earthsiders alike. It will be a feather in their caps as well as mine to know that a child of Martian heredity has been reclaimed to the planet of his ancestors!"

Now at last his tone did change, and rose with excitement as he clapped me on the shoulder. "Ray, I've had pupils I thought were better than you—more attentive, more interested—but this I swear: I never hoped to be taught by any of them! And you've shown me how blind I was, thanks to my own traditions."

Yetta leaned forward. "So what are you going to do?"

"Go find the child with maximum publicity!" Thoder exclaimed, and started for the door. "We believe him to be somewhere in this college, most likely in Jives's quarters, where the crying of a child would be nothing extraordinary. A great many young Bear couples—often graduate students —come back here to take a short course when their children are born, thinking that luck is something that can be soaked out of the air and absorbed into the babies' bones!"

"Is this idea deliberately encouraged?" I asked, thinking of the weird woman with the polychrome hair who'd challenged us.

"Of course—it maximises the contrast between Bear and Centaur to have one society rigidly pre-planned, the other cheerfully accepting randomness as a major factor in life."

As we hurried down the long walkways linking the main college building to the smaller one where the Bear students were housed, I was so relieved I'd almost turned off my mind. I glanced at the wall-decorations, seeing how they repeated the same theme as was represented on the exterior of the domes: games of chance, lucky and unlucky symbols. Some of them were of curious archeological interest, such as the picture of a room containing a broken mirror, vases of flowers which Earthsiders traditionally considered of ill-omen, bunches of peacock's feathers, spilled salt and crossed cutlery lying on a table—even, so help me, an umbrella which had been opened inside the house. I wondered if an umbrella had ever been brought to Mars; I'd never seen one until I landed for the first time on Charigol in a rain-storm.

We made no attempt either to attract or to avoid attention, and a good many people saw us pass, mostly Bear students dispersing to their rooms in the same dome as Jives. My closing-down mind ignored them.

It was only the chance of my walking more quickly than the elderly Thoder, thanks to which I rechanced the junction of three passageways and paused with a glance in either direction while waiting for him to catch up with me, that I spotted him. It was only a glimpse as he dodged out of sight, but it snapped me back into full relationship with the present.

I gasped. Yetta, who had been walking more slowly than I out of politeness towards Thoder, closed the gap between us and demanded to know what was wrong.

I said, "I just saw Peter Nizam! What can he be doing here?" And answered my own question in the same breath: "Cosmos! Of course, Lilith Choy recognised me in the cab on the way here!"

Thoder paled. "But that's not the way to Jives's room!" he rapped. He waved down the passage opposite to that in which I'd seen Peter, and broke into a stumbling run.

It was abundantly clear, the moment we thrust open the door of Jives's quarters, that Peter had put two and two together and come to warn Jives to make himself scarce. There was no one here, but there had been. The door of a closet swung ajar, and there was the smell of a wet baby within it.

"One of these days," Yetta said very softly, "I'm going to tell what I think of people who will treat a child as a kind of parcel—trade-goods, to be swapped around from hand to hand. And that includes you, uncle."

"Which way could they have gone?" I demanded. "Is there an exit the way Nizam went?"

"No, but you can go through another dome and take a passage back to the entrance!"

"Try and cut them off!" Yetta said. I nodded and ran from the room.

This time, the people I encountered were sufficiently intrigued to come after me—not at my speed, but in a gaggle of curiosity. I stormed into the same hallway where I'd encountered the woman with the incredible hair, and there she was again, holding forth to a group of middle-aged students on the dreadful intrusion she'd witnessed. Seeing me, she broke off with her hand to her mouth.

"Did Jives come this way?" I snapped at her. She didn't answer, but moaned and swayed with eyes closed, doubtless imagining her private castle of luck collapsing as in an earthquake.

I would learn nothing from the astonished and dismayed students, I could be sure of that. I dashed to the window alongside the main entrance, peering out to see if there was anyone there resembling either Jives or Peter.

And there was! A short distance away, not having suckled up as a cab would have done to connect directly with the higher pressure of the building, stood a private car, something very rare on Mars. Racing towards it were two men. One looked like Peter, the other—burdened with an oblong bundle which I recognised as a pressurised baby-carrier—was Jives.

I went into extended time faster than I'd ever managed it before, and went so deep that my mask felt heavy as lead when I forced it over my face. Even my body felt sluggish, as I'm told it does in water on an Earthlike world; Martian to the marrow of my bones, I'd never attempted to swim. Nonetheless I managed to get through the door and outside, head ringing from the sudden rise in my oxygen intake as I clumsily mis-adjusted the cylinder feeding my mask.

Though I couldn't see through the car's windows, I was sure Lilith must be on board, waiting for the split-second after her companions' arrival to drive off at high speed. The mere use of extended time would never have brought me up to them before that; it took another chance factor operating in my favour to delay them. A car designed for Mars work—or a truck, or anything—couldn't carry a building-sized airlock or the air-supply needed to refill it each time it cycled. The lock, therefore, consisted in a man-sized compartment with flush sliding doors, from which the air was driven by inflated plastic sheets, contouring themselves to the occupant as the two doors cycled. I'd complained of the way all Mars vehicles seemed to be scaled to Earthside midgets. For once I was grateful that this was so.

The bulk of the baby-carrier meant that the lock had to be operated three times, not twice; that Nizam had to go in first, wait to receive the baby inside the lock, and then make way for Jives.

I caught up just as the lock was opening for the baby, shouting. Jives heard me despite the bad sound-conduction of this natural exterior air, turned and saw me racing towards him, stood for a long second in petrified horror, and took to his heels, baby and all.

My detour into extended time had to stop here; I wasn't capable of using oxygen at the rate needed to support such frantic double-speed activity, and I'd got this far on the "second wind" of a long-distance runner. Nonetheless my heart gave an exultant bound. Jives might be able to get away from me briefly, using his high-gravity musculature, but I could wear him down with my loping Martian strides and drive him into soft patches of sand where he would flounder helplessly while I—big-footed, accustomed to the conditions—would have the superiority of a camel over a horse in an Earthside desert.

That became clear to him too after only a short distance. Thinking he'd outpaced me, he paused and glanced back, and saw me still coming on, running lightly and easily where he was struggling.

Dismay showed plainly on the part of his face not covered by his mask; his windchapped forehead ridged in a frown of alarm. Suddenly he bent to set down the baby-carrier, and I thought he was going to surrender, for he didn't simply let it fall and abandon it, but stayed leaning over it for several seconds.

Then, unexpectedly, he darted off again at right angles, and I was on the point of cutting the corners of the route and making straight towards him, when something clicked in the back of my mind and I made for the baby instead.

It wasn't possible—was it? No Bear could do that in cold blood. A Centaur, yes, but . . .

And he *had* done it. I could tell while I was still twenty paces away. He'd disconnected the air-cylinder on the side of the baby-carrier, and it was whistling its oxygen uselessly into nowhere, while the baby gasped and cried for breath.

I dropped on my knees with a cry, hands feverish to restore the connection. It was too late already. The valve was open to its fullest extent, and since it had been designed to feed the contents into the carrier against a normal pressure of zero Earthside feet the few moments since it had been exposed to Martian pressure of a hundred thousand had sufficed to drain the entire contents.

I stared bleakly at the child's contorted face under the transparent cover of the carrier. Through smeared condensation I could see he was panting furiously. There was enough oxygen in the carrier to sustain him a little longer, but these things were bulky enough already, and waste space was reduced to a minimum.

There was only one thing to do, and I did it almost without thinking. I closed the valve on my own mask's cylinder after taking several deep breaths, disconnected it, and coupled it awkwardly to the hose dangling from the carrier. The fittings, of course, were standardised, but they seemed to resent being screwed together; my head was swimming before I could open the valve again.

I looked to see how the baby's breathing had eased, my eyes blurred. I glanced around me once, seeing that Jives had circled back towards the ridiculous gaudy domes of the college, that even yet no one else had had time to mask up and emerge from there in pursuit of me, that the car with Peter and Lilith was stopping to pick up Jives and get him away . . .

Then I put myself into contracted time, and the whole world melted in a blur of redness.

XXI

I WASN'T SURE I was going to come back from that zone of distorted time. Later, often, I wished that I need not, but could rest for eternity in a blanket of silence. For I returned to nausea, pain, a delirious chaos of mental images into which occasionally broke real events that I could not isolate and recognise. Sometimes I thought that I myself was a child again, trapped and struggling for breath—this might have been the memory of a trauma I'd actually experienced when I was being accustomed to Martian standard air after leaving the clinic where I was born. Then, of course, I was sure I'd failed in my attempt to save the baby's life, that my clumsy fingers had misconnected the air-cylinder or that I'd blacked out before I could open the valve. If that were so I didn't want to come back to awareness and face my shame.

Abruptly it was all over, and I was weak but whole, lying in a quiet twilit room surrounded by bouquets of sandflowers in protected vases, against each of which lay a little white card. The first thing I saw clearly when I awoke from my final feverish slumber was such a card, and on it read:

To Ray in sincere admiration. Yetta.

I rolled my head, and there was an Earthside girl, rather fat, in a nurse's uniform. She smiled and asked how I felt and inspected some instruments connected to my wrists and temples by fine wires, and said I was going to get better very quickly now.

But beyond assuring me that the baby had survived, she wouldn't tell me any of the things I wanted to know. I lay fretting until I drifted into sleep again.

The first visitor I was allowed to receive, the first person of whom I could demand information, was Lugath, and he had changed. Gone were the last traces of his Centaur stiffness; he wore mismatched casual clothes and he'd let his hair grow out of its Centaur officer's crop. He looked ill at ease notwithstanding, as if some basic prop had been withdrawn from his life.

I plied him with questions, and he responded absently. "Oh—yes, it all seems to have gone as you planned. Jives? They're going to try him for attempted murder, and pro-Bear sentiment has gone down all over the Old System, not only on Mars. Nizam and his girl friend? Oh, apparently the pro-Bear organisation which they were working for has had such a rash of resignations it's likely to go bankrupt, and I don't know what's become of them. They hadn't done anything criminal, of course, so . . .

"Housk? It's because of him, they tell me, that Yetta

couldn't stay here until you recovered. She wanted to, I gather, but she had this blazing row with her uncle over the way we were treating a helpless baby, and—you know something? I think she was right. She was throwing all Thoder's own precepts at him, in private of course because it would have ruined the impact of public sympathy which your picture of him as a wronged grandparent generated . . .

"But I was telling you about Housk. She had to go back to Pegasus and clear up the mess there. Her chief—Dr Snell —seems to be a tough character, and apparently there was some real ill-feeling among the Martians on the staff of his clinic, so it wasn't just a matter of turning Housk back to his own people and letting them deal with him. There's an interstellar diplomatic crisis boiling out of it. But it'll pass, I guess. She took the kid with her, by the way; declared she was better fitted to look after him than Thoder, and of course she was right. One of the finest maternity clinics on Mars, they say . . .

"The Old Temple? Yes, of course it was because Housk was sneering at it that the Martian staff of the clinic got so angry. I'd never realised how much it meant to you people, but obviously it meant enough for people not to want to ask awkward questions about it. It's been a sort of fairy story, hasn't it? Like—what the hell did they call him?— Santa Claus. And his reindeer! I'm almost beginning to share their feelings myself, these days.

"Hadn't you realised? Ray, I'm sorry! I'd have thought you would already have caught on. I'm going to have to settle in the Old System permanently. I can't go back to flying space, and that's been my life. The Bears won't have me, because they know perfectly well I wasn't a Bear agent even if the Centaurs think I was, and naturally since the Centaurs do think so they won't have me either. I'm *persona non grata* on every human planet north and south of Old System, and so, incidentally, are you.

"But you're lucky. At least you do have a home world to come back to. Do you realise I haven't set foot on Earth in thirty-two years? How much of a home does that make it for me? And yet I guess it's not much of a price to pay, if we can bring up that kid and his kids in their turn to disregard unimportant labels like Centaur and Bear and Earthsider and Martian . . .

"I'm sorry I had to be the one to break the truth to you, but I honestly did think you'd realised already!"

I should have done, of course. In my weakened state I railed against it, though. Oh, there were ships under Earth registry as well as Centaur and Bear—I could work for an Earthside line and still fly space. But the only planets I'd be allowed to move about on would be Earth and Mars, and everywhere else I'd be refused permission to land. What use was a life like that? So my career was gone.

In its place—what? A drab deadend existence like my father's? My eyes roved the little cards on the bouquets of flowers, in the hope that they would cheer me up. All kinds of people had apparently been impressed by what I'd done, in the distorted form in which it was circulated, some of whom I'd never heard of, some of whom I wouldn't have expected to take the trouble. Gus Quaison, for example.

And my father. Must go see him. No more thinking that Thoder was my effective father. After all, he'd revealed himself without realising as just as much of a prisoner of circumstances as anyone else. All humans had to admit that.

When Thoder did come to see me, I didn't give him a very warm welcome. He sensed my resentment and sat down in silence facing the bed, as if put out by the reception he was having.

I let him wonder at it until he decided to speak first.

"Ray, are you holding some grudge against me? Is it because of what Lugath told you? He said you didn't seem to realise that because of this affair neither you nor he nor any others of his crew will be permitted to—"

"No, it's not that. Or that doesn't account for very much of it." I passed a weary hand over my eyes. "I've been lying here and thinking, and I've come to a conclusion. I think the same way Yetta does about people who treat a living human child as a sort of gaming-chip."

He hesitated. At length he said, "But reflect a little further, Ray. Do you resent being a Martian?"

"Hell, no. And I think I have rational grounds for being proud that I am!"

"Yet you were deliberately made into a Martian, long before you were born. The shape of Martian society was planned for. Things you're proud of—honour, traditional ways of behaviour—weren't randomly evolved, but part of a grand blueprint for human evolution."

"Maybe that was the bit that came out all right. The rest—" I made a face. "Bears? I thought they were pretty good people, but Jives is a Bear and he was capable of turning off a baby's oxygen for no better reason than that he knew Centaurs were keen to reclaim him. Earthsiders? Peter and Lilith are Earthsiders, and they were willing to kidnap and smuggle away the child. Centaurs reek in everybody's nostrils, and when you come down to it there are Martians who are willing to let their own granddaughters—"

"Ray!" In abrupt anger, Thoder leaned forward. "You accused me of being blinded by my Martian conditioning into clinging to secrecy when I could have relied on public sympathy and—and hit on your own solution to our problem. I admitted the charge. I'm now bringing it against you in your turn. Haven't you lived a casual, easy-going, _immoral_ life during stopovers on Bear planets? Haven't you enjoyed plenty of girls without calling them harsh names? Shilene is a grown woman in a child's body, consciously dedicated to a scheme she will never see bear fruit. If I hadn't believed this was how it would turn out, do you think I'd have let her be caught up in it?

"Yetta informs me that when Housk taunted Martians for believing in the reality of the Old Temple as a native relic you described in a flash of insight the purpose it served for us—the noble lie, the splendid myth which everyone realises is true on a symbolic level. You said your Martian ancestors were willing to die billions of miles from home for the sake of their children's children. Are you going to mock someone who's doing the same, because it so happens she has to choose a different _kind_ of dedication? And because it infringes your narrow-minded Martian double standards?"

I couldn't answer. He gave me the chance to speak, then continued. "We were talking about aims and ideals, weren't we? About human destiny? You said you accepted that each generation had to select its own version and be prepared to see the next generation revise it. Well, the same damned thing applies to the ethics which reflect the ideal. I wish it didn't. I wish I was primitive enough to accept some kind of revelatory dogma and shut up. But 'for all that we graph 'progress' in terms of starships and mental patients, we're tied to the assumption that we aren't shut in an enclosed cycle which repeats and repeats and drags us helplessly up and down forever, but at worst in a sort of maze, which may have a way out and certainly has paths in it that we haven't yet traversed. If for no more valid reason than that—well—that it makes a change of scenery and saves us from boredom, I like it better the second way. And when we get to the point at which we can't discover a new turning to explore, then what else are we to do if not create the sort of human beings who *will* be able to?"

After a pause, I said, "Yes. Maybe. Oh, I guess you're right. But meantime I have a life of my own to live, and I don't know what to do with it now my career's gone and I can't return to space. Which is why I'm snapping at you."

Thoder hesitated. He said finally, "I mentioned this to Yetta, who's at least as remarkable a person as anyone else in my family. And I'll tell you what she said.

"She said, 'Go back to space? Do you think he'll want to? Now he knows all the things you've told him, don't you expect that he'll want a part of it, starting with what comes to hand in the shape of this kid likely to grow into a man who will change history?' I shan't live forever, Ray. And as a very apt pupil of mine, I imagine you may feel that some of the things I've tried to teach you ought to form part of the boy's education. I don't know anyone who's applied my precepts more successfully, and that's the truth . . ."

He rose, smiling. "Think it over," he said. "And when you make your mind up, tell Yetta, will you? She seemed rather —ah—eager to have her idea confirmed."

So I did.

And she was.

CLASSICS OF GREAT SCIENCE-FICTION

from ACE BOOKS